THE CHINESE MANSION

Praise for the book

'Like the enigmatic writings of Naiyer Masud, *The Chinese Mansion* pulls us into a mysterious narrative where elusive subtexts always seem to flutter beneath the surface, just out of reach, and Jaideep Pandey masterfully maintains the mystery in his arrestingly clear translation.' – **Daisy Rockwell, award-winning translator of *Tomb of Sand***

Praise for the Urdu edition

'Successfully employs surrealism to access innermost experience and emotional trajectory – the heart, mind and creative process.' **– Mehr Afshan Farooqi, author of *Ghalib: A Wilderness at My Doorstep***

'[In *Cheeni Kothi*] new facets of existence constantly discard or put on makeshift meanings, and it is illusion which threatens to become real.' – **M. Salim-ur-Rehman, author and translator**

THE CHINESE MANSION

SIDDIQUE ALAM

Translated from the Urdu by Jaideep Pandey

hachette INDIA

First published in Urdu as *Cheeni Kothi* in 2016 by Arshia Publications, Delhi

This translation first published in 2025 by Hachette India
(Registered name: Hachette Book Publishing India Pvt. Ltd)
An Hachette UK company
www.hachetteindia.com

1

Cover design and illustration by Harshavardhan Behura

Print ISBN 978-93-5731-526-5
eBook ISBN 978-93-5731-801-3

Hachette Book Publishing India Pvt. Ltd
4th & 5th Floors, Corporate Centre,
Plot No. 94, Sector 44, Gurugram 122003, India

Typeset in EB Garamond 11.5/16
by R. Ajith Kumar, New Delhi

Printed and bound in India
by Thomson Press India Ltd.

MIX
Paper | Supporting responsible forestry
FSC
www.fsc.org
FSC® C010615

Useless oars never cross a river

– Shu Ting's poem 'Missing You'

Translator's Preface

CREDITED WITH CULTIVATING A HIGHLY SYMBOLIC, surrealistic and experimental style in Urdu prose fiction, Siddique Alam (b. 1952 in Purulia, West Bengal) is one of the most important contemporary voices to have graced Urdu fiction in India.. Alam published his first collection of short stories, *Aakhri Chhaon* (Last Shade) in 1982. It was followed by a long hiatus, broken with the publication of his first work of prose poetry *Charnok Ki Kashti* (The Four Pointed Boat), in 2003, on the landscape of Kolkata, followed by collections of short stories, *Lamp Jalane Waalay* (The People Who Light the Lamp) in 2007, and *Bain* (Mourning) in 2012.

The Chinese Mansion was published in Urdu as *Cheeni Kothi*, in 2016, to widespread critical acclaim. Alam followed the success of the novel by entering the most prolific period of his literary career, publishing a short story collection, *Marey Hue Admi Ki Laltein* (The Dead Man's Lantern, 2019), two novels – *Saliha, Saliha* and *Marzboom* (Native Land, 2021) – and another short story collection, *Nadir Sikkon Ka Baks* (A Box of Rare Coins, 2022), followed by two more novels – *Bioscope Wala* and *Marg-e Dawam* (Eternal Death, 2024).

Alam belongs to a new generation of experimental Urdu writers – along with Naiyer Masud, Shamsur Rahman Faruqi and Khalid Jawed from India, and Mirza Athar Baig and Syed Kashif Raza from Pakistan – who began their literary careers in the long aftermath of the mid-20th century – appearance of avant-garde literary trends in Urdu, captured in the term *jadidiyat,* or literary modernism. Avant-garde trends appeared in Urdu literature as a rebellion against demands of clarity and incisive social realism created by the earlier movement – the Progressive Writers' Association (PWA). Modernism instead emphasized the *alaamati kahani* (symbolic story) and declared an open revolt against established conventions and rules for literary composition by relying on complex symbols and obscure and layered use of language and metaphors that sought to challenge and confound the readers' comprehension. While it would be reductive to say that this was an opposition between political versus aesthetic functions of literature, modernism and the PWA followed two different understandings of language and its power in relation to the world that it sought to describe. Farhat Ehsas aptly describes this as a battle between *pabandi* (regulation) and *azadi* (freedom), between the *mahdood* (limited) and the *la mahdood* (unlimited).

Alam's work attempts a truce of sorts. His prose is grounded firmly in specific socio-political realities of eastern India – particularly Bengal – and draws on local caste politics, language debates and class structures to paint a heavily layered world and the complex structures of power that produce it. At the same time, however, his novels and short stories are impressionistic, and experiment with forms, perceptions of realities, and ways of communicating meaning and emotions to readers. To this end, Alam's novelistic worlds demand an active reader, one who is willing to continuously engage and participate with the world of his prose, where meaning is made through a play with language, a sharp yet distorted perception of reality, and a wide range of malleability around the notion of 'event' in narrative fiction. Large stretches of Alam's novels follow his appreciation of Chekhov's style where nothing happens, but everything happens. So, in this overwhelming lack of conventional 'events', Alam expects the reader to plunge deep into the labyrinth of emotions and experiences of reality that shape the world of his characters, to actively pick up strands and structures of meaning. Alam achieves a sort of truce between the specificity of the PWA and the non-specificity or openness of modernism, by relying heavily on the unconscious of both the writer and the reader to craft a world where they communicate with each other in landscapes shaped mutually by their conscious and unconscious minds. This communication is often not direct or clear, but through cryptic symbols, which make the world of the novel both specific, but at the same time, infinitely expansive, and open to interpretive possibilities.

Another hallmark of Alam's literary oeuvre is his belief that 'humans have forcibly occupied the entire planet', and his subsequent interest in animals, landscapes and the non-human. Alam rejects the human claim of being *ashraf al-makhlooqat* or the most honoured of all creations, instead thinks of them as occupiers consumed with violent instincts. Animals appear frequently in his work bearing the brunt of human violence and egocentrism. A very clear example of this is the storyline of the cat, Payal, in this book. His world also goes beyond animals to include pieces of land, trees and rivers, all of which suffer under our anthropocentric imaginations. Alam's novels thus force characters and readers alike to confront the limits to their imagination and read for the silences and emotions that the novels' landscapes breathe. He shares this tendency with his contemporaries such as Naiyer Masud's interest in birds, Khalid Jawed's interest in archaeology, or Rahman Abbas's interest in natural disasters.

Combining elements of surrealism, magic realism and absurdism, *The Chinese Mansion* sketches out a picture of the terrifying dark corners of everyday life in small-town eastern India. The novel takes a hard philosophical look at how caste, gender and legal processes structure encounters with questions of life, death, trauma, morality and deep-seated bigotry in the South Asian countryside. It follows the life and career of our protagonist, a lawyer, through five seemingly unrelated plot lines that become symbolically linked through the narrator's consciousness. The first is his obsession with the titular Chinese mansion, which is next to the lawyer's house. Inhabited by a Chinese family for a long time, the house is the center of town gossip ripe with unserious though malevolent racist speculations and stereotypes. The protagonist is obsessed with what goes on inside the mansion, even as he acknowledges the deep prejudices and bigotry against the Chinese that he grew up with. The second is a court case involving the rape of an eight-year-old girl by a forty-year-old man in a village located close to the protagonist's town. Alam's protagonist is the defence lawyer for the rape-accused and even as he slowly realizes the accusation to be true, he continues to fight for him through the legal circus that unfolds in the courtroom. The third is another client named Aisha, who is an attractive, widowed mother of three and has employed the protagonist as her lawyer in a long-drawn family property dispute. Aisha and the protagonist develop a relationship, much to the anger of her eighteen-year-old son, Nadir, who tries to stalk and chase him away. The fourth is his reticent friendship with a retired police officer whom he encounters in his daily strolls along the riverbanks that flank the town. The retired policeman, who lives alone, is depressed as he looks for his adopted cat, Payal, who disappeared a few weeks ago. While the protagonist is initially dismissive of this quest, he becomes more and more drawn to its morbid details as the novel progresses. The fifth is the protagonist's relationship with his staff – Hiranmoy, a Bengali clerk who assists the protagonist in court cases and suffers from a difficult family life and a deluded 'upper caste' pride; and Mir, an erstwhile Naxal who was accused of killing his wife and child. The protagonist had unsuccessfully defended Mir in court, and after serving his prison sentence, has been the caretaker of the domestic affairs of the former's house. All these psycho-sexual negotiations are set against the protagonist's troubled family history, and the novel brings together these plots to produce a powerful meditation on loss, trauma, death and transformations.

The storytelling sees a mix of genres. It often reads as courtroom drama, given that the protagonist is a lawyer, and the reader is brought uncomfortably close to the goings-on of several of his cases. It also reads as a star-crossed romance between Aisha and the protagonist, soon to reveal the deeply troubling currents of sexual attraction that form their tumultuous relationship. Most importantly, however, the novel is an urban chronicle of small-town India, which comes alive for the readers in minute historical details of the caste, class and gender politics that crisscross the characters' relationships with each other as well as with the city's geography. Alam's chronicle explores the Indian small town through the dreamlike and phantasmagorical visions that haunt it, beyond history and reason, guided by the increasingly unreliable and morally murky mind of the central character.

The Chinese Mansion was acclaimed by Urdu readers and critics across India and Pakistan alike upon its release, and has already seen multiple reprints and editions since 2016. Mehr Afshan Farooqi, Associate Professor in the Department of

Middle Eastern and South Asian Languages and Cultures at the University of Virginia, hailed the novel for how it 'successfully employs surrealism to access innermost experience and emotional trajectory – the heart, mind and creative process'. The Pakistani literary critic M. Salim-Ur-Rehman compared Alam's style to the giant of modern Urdu prose, Naiyer Masud, and said that in his work, 'new facets of existence constantly discard or put on makeshift meanings, and it is illusion which threatens to become real.' In 2023, the Hindi translation of *The Chinese Mansion* by the veteran translator and professor, Arjumand Ara was shortlisted for the Bank of Baroda Rashtrabhasha Samman Award.

Translating Alam's work was a humbling experience in working with language for me. On the surface, his prose is presented in a straightforward style where language exists as a transparent medium that describes buildings, landscapes and everyday actions. However, the dangerous stillness of his language and landscape slowly pulls in the reader into a world teetering at the edge of physical, psychological and semantic catastrophe, one which fully implicates the reader through its strategy of placing the onus of finding the unreal, the uncanny and the awry on them. Several parts of the novel are written in present tense, which draw the reader quietly into the moment of action, until they inhabit the landscape of the writer's and characters' unconscious. This balance between the placid and the truly unsettling was the biggest challenge in translating Alam's prose. I have attempted to keep the English as unobtrusive as the Urdu original, to allow the reader to invite themselves into the interpretive capaciousness of the text. At the same time, the Urdu original employs extensive caste-, race- and gender-biased vocabulary to allow the readers to fully confront these structures within this interpretive capaciousness. I have kept these terms as they are in the English to avoid sanitizing the landscape of the novel riddled with prejudices of various kinds.

For me as a translator and reader, the immense value of *The Chinese Mansion* lies in its ability to make us contemplate the nature of violence, sex and prejudices that structure our worldviews, even when we are at our unassuming best. This contemplation is fostered by the novel's seemingly nondescript and neutral language where the writer, translator and reader can come together in one shared emotional landscape, to communicate with each other through one's own conscious and unconscious predispositions towards desire and catastrophe. My translation is an attempt to preserve this quality of the original, where reading and translating become a way of achieving an uncomfortably deep intimacy with characters, their worldviews, and shared histories that threaten to blow the cover of calmness that we weave around our worlds.

Chapter One

WAVING ITS TAIL FROM SIDE TO SIDE WHILE ROLLING its eyeballs in its sockets, it would always materialize in the same fashion, either from behind the cluster of fuzzy stars or piercing through the moonlit clouds. Occasionally, its craggy jaw would drop open with teeth glinting like crooked icicles. An animal it was, shaped almost like a dragon, though not fully one. Or perhaps it really was a dragon, but instead of flames, its mouth would emit jets of steam. When he had first spotted the creature eight years back, he was only ten years old. On that day too, he had seen it from under the same window curtain, which was billowing out in the same manner as it billows today as he looks at it from his bed set against the wall, his elbows piercing the pillow, his face cupped in his palms. The sky was overcast that day, but there are no clouds today. There is only a light haze on the horizon, and the creature is struggling not to become one with it. It does not take long to gain in stature, as if it is gradually coming closer to the earth. Right then, he hears a hard, muffled thud at the door, and a man stumbles into the room. His bald head is sweating profusely, wisps of hair sticking out of earlobes, shirt buttons undone and eyes bloodshot. Together, they give him a frazzled look. The man flops on the bed and hugs him. As the man kisses his forehead, his lips tremble. The boy is not used to these outbursts. They rarely cross each other's paths. Why is it then that the man has suddenly become so emotional, sticking his head out of his lair? *It is nothing but a nightmare,* the man is repeating over and over. *Why don't you try to give sleep a chance? You aren't usually up at this odd hour.*

To get rid of him, the boy shuts his eyes, and the dragon pops up in the canopy of his eyelids, more vivid than before.

He has no idea how much time has passed. He opens his eyes as he hears a crackling sound on the staircase outside. He is alone in his bed. The sound vanishes. Once again, he looks at the sky. That dragon is still there, stuck at the same spot. But now, its eyes have acquired an icy coldness while its body is gradually growing faint. Its eyes shine one last time, and it is gone. He hasn't even been able to shake off its afterimage from his retina when he hears a loud explosion from the floor below.

Two dogs emerged from behind the Chinese Mansion, fighting loudly and bitterly, robbing me of my sleep. But am I really awake, or am I seeing these two dogs having this brawl in my dream? What is the matter with the Chinese Mansion that it blurs the line between dream and reality? What is so special about this mansion, except that its old, latticed windows below the three-cornered roof of country tiles always remain shut while the puny birds perched atop the telephone and electric lines between the gate and the house try to be as invisible as possible until they soar in the air to swap positions? The stone pillars of the gate support a lintel topped with country tiles. The left pillar has a large, square alcove – god knows for what arcane purpose! – its corners darkened by cobwebs. The right pillar has a lamp bracket jutting out of it, the remains of an iron cage resembling a rat's snout. At some point in time, coloured glass must have adorned it, framing it on all sides, to allow a kerosene wick to maintain its flame. Now, this cage is empty. The fact is, as far as I can remember, I have always seen it in the form of a cage. Made from cast-iron and shorn of its original colour due to the vagaries of weather, it stands as a relic of a golden past. The pigeons, who sit still on the wooden ornaments of the roof or take shelter in the narrow skylights or hide under the eaves with their wooden teeth slanting downwards, are always bewitched by their own cooing while one or two of them can be seen draping the lamp bracket with their white or chequered wings.

Once, in my dream, I noticed a bird, mandarin red in colour, the size of an eagle, perched atop it. Waking up, I wondered how I could see it there in its full splendour when such birds are conspicuous by their absence in our country. To be honest, I doubt its very existence! Was this on account of those loud colours with which the Chinese usually paint their walls that this bird had imprinted itself in my dream? It was difficult for me to figure out whether I was sleeping or awake, as the clouds had transformed the day into night while a gale kept sweeping the rain across the road as if it were a sort of fog, not to speak of another draft that kept spraying rainwater through the window into my room. I was about to close the shutter when my gaze fell on the wooden gate of the Chinese Mansion, whose gold paint had disappeared long ago. It was flung wide open, and a chocolate-coloured coffin was being brought out. My eyes instinctively went up to the lamp bracket. No red bird was there. In its place, a plastic Chinese lantern was hanging from an electric wire, swaying to one side like a balloon. With the light coming out of the mandarin red paper, the wooden door and the adjoining walls bore a bizarre look as if blood was dripping on them. Beams of light from innumerable torches danced in the opening at the gateway. The light of dry cell torches fused together, forming dark and hazy human silhouettes, silhouettes intermingling, criss-crossing, getting stuck and separating to their original shapes. Some of these human silhouettes, holding umbrellas in their hands, were opening and closing vehicle doors. It mystified me to see Chinese people rally there in such a large number.

Had people of Chinese origin taken over this small city?

Maybe they had travelled this far from neighbouring towns to attend the funeral, I reassured myself. But why was I standing in front of the window, getting drenched for no reason? Did it matter to me who was being carried away in the coffin when I knew that, in the end, some or the other Chinese would remain in our town?

I don't know anyone from the Chinese Mansion. The only Chinese dentist in our town has his clinic on Station Road, and the skylight above its large entrance is always shut and foggy. We children would always be terrified by this skylight. Whenever we had occasion to pass by the place, we would imagine children screaming and wailing inside the clinic as their teeth were being pulled out by the unrelenting Chinese holding sharp pincers in their scraggy hands. We would hear these screams even when the glass door of the clinic was wide open, giving the clinic an empty and quiet look. The dentures and toothless gums, arranged in a row in the display windows, would look like they had been wrenched out of the jaws of demons. The truth was, we would always take them for real things. Though I never had a chance to go to this Chinese dentist, I had once seen him up close, when he was travelling in his personal rickshaw. He was swaying sideways, holding the pipes in his firm grip lest he topple down, though, at that time, he was swaying more under the influence of liquor than the rickshaw's jerky movements. Now and then, he would keep batting around his hand to drive away some imaginary fly that was trying to land on his smooth, hairless skull. With the road going uphill, the rickshaw was crawling at a snail's pace, and riding my bicycle next to him, I felt like we both had stopped at the same place. His cauliflower ears were too large, and a big mole sat on the right side of his chin, drooping downwards under the weight of its own pressure. A few strands of hair grew out of that mole. He had slits in the name of eyes, and his face looked like a mango sucked dry, leaving no juice inside. His eyes would rarely open, but once they did, they would remain open for eternity. His lower jaw was completely ossified, as if someone had pulled it off a dead body that had been buried long ago and had stitched it there. He only needed to open the jaw to let tiny birds the size of tinkles fly out of his mouth, chirping loudly as if they had gone mad. Although I had grown up right in front of the Chinese Mansion, we were so terrified of its doors and permanently shut windows that we never dared to peep inside. For us, the Chinese people hailed from a mysterious land that always lay buried in mist, and according to what we had heard from our elders, they worshipped their forefathers as if they were gods and goddesses. They ate all sorts of things, including snakes and frogs, and deftly rode dragons over hills and jungles. We had grown up with these prejudices and bigotry against the Chinese.

Finally, the coffin was placed in a white hearse, torches were switched off one after another, and the cars started to move bumper to bumper, vanishing in the foggy rain. A man had been left behind in the last receding light of a torch, struggling with the gate against the rain, which had gained momentum. Finally, the gate was closed, and with it, the force of the wind abated. The Chinese lantern became still as its wire fell into a straight line, restored to its original position. The exterior of the gate was lit up by the lantern, with the shadows of pillars falling on the adjoining walls, rendering them invisible. The lanterns continued to be bathed in the rain for a while, and then, they were switched off. With all the lights gone, the entrance of the Chinese Mansion should have vanished in the darkness, but the wooden gate and both its pillars, as also the adjoining walls, all became visible. I remove my fingers from the icy cold window and look out at the sky, where the sunlight made inroads through the crevices of clouds, as if someone poured hot, molten lava through them. I am surprised when I find what I mistook for night was, in fact, a bright day, a significant part of it still extant. The rain stops. Someone calls my name from inside the house. I realize the birds might wake up any time and start chirping in the ruined garden. But silence prevails for a long time, and the sunlight gradually extinguishes itself into the crevices of clouds.

The rain starts again...

A river flows next to our city. Its banks on both sides are covered by dense forests, interspersed with fallow lands. These are overrun with thistles and prickly bushes, all abodes of snakes and scorpions. The riverbed, at some points, has spread out to almost half a mile or more which, barring the rainy months, remains dry throughout the year as if it were a desert, except for those thin streams of water that cut across the sand like sharp knives. These streams flow forward in a disorderly manner, sometimes flowing against their own directions. Thickets of rushes stand lush and tall on the marshy land on the city side. On fine mornings, clucking jungle hens can be seen roaming about there. One can even see all sorts of migratory birds descend from the sky onto the marshland. With the scarcity of water, these reeds dry up during the summer. Standing twisted and moribund, they look entangled and interlaced as if they are supporting one another. Stray dogs flock there to hunt down the wild hens, but it isn't easy to find them in the dense overgrowth, which is also the arena where life-and-death fights occur between mongooses and snakes. This marsh is, in fact, fed by the waste water that sewage pipes pour into the river, giving the place the look of a temporary dam. Even though 'Bhangis' regularly clean out the concrete drains and ditches that run into the river. The trash they dredge up and leave behind not only rots and dries up but, over a period of time, drifts back to the dry riverbed, until the biggest cleanser of the universe, the monsoon, arrives with its mission of cleaning up the mess. It is then time for the river to wake up like a monster and spread out. Its massive watery arms carry away all the garbage awaiting disposal at the bank. But the riverbank does not have the same look everywhere. In some places, there are bars of sand between rocks that are clean and dry where one can take a safe stroll. Here, birds chirp, squirrels run around, dogs, who have only God as their master, bark, and donkeys, no longer needed by washermen, philosophically laze around, a breed that has somehow kept itself alive, maintaining their lineage against all odds. But that day isn't far when, like all other things no longer needed by human beings, these donkeys will also vanish from the earth. The river, however, isn't just confined to these things. If you take a walk up the river, trees, bushes and beautiful rocks will emerge from nowhere, where you can rest or lose yourself in a daydream, or you can see smoke across the river rise from the village huts with eagles and crows descending upon them, or you can hear *azan* from some nearby mosques, or temple bells, which aren't hard on the ears because of the distance. No wonder it will compel you to close your eyes and fantasize that perhaps the world is getting along just fine and that we hold on to our long list of grievances for no reason whatsoever.

It is here that one day, I met a retired police sub-inspector, a confirmed bachelor, who, having lost his cat, was in a very sombre mood. The first time I saw him, a stubborn fly was trying doggedly to settle down on his snuff box. Perhaps his nasal fluid had permanently congealed on its lid.

'You can go for a dog,' I proposed by way of light humour since I was sure I had a lot of things to say in favour of a dog as an ideal pet. We had taken shelter under a tree. A dog is a faithful animal that can even sacrifice his life for you. They are so loyal that they won't even bark if you ask them not to. Moreover, people say that they even warn you of an imminent earthquake before it actually takes place. But you can't say the same thing about a cat. Cats are selfish. They have their own dubious world to fall back to where human beings have no access.

'When they come close to a man, it is not because they are fond of him, but because they think the man might have something useful for them. It's not that nature hasn't endowed cats with any special qualities. Their canines are not only very pointy, their nails are extremely sharp too. They have an acute sense of smell that is even stronger than dog's, and they can see in pitch-darkness. But what's the use? Despite these qualities, they aren't any help to mankind.'

He regarded me with alarm.

'You can't say that. Payal was a very faithful cat. Is it necessary that we should look at everything from the point of view of its utility?' he said, shooing away the fly from his snuff box. 'I can say with full confidence that she is a faithful cat. Maybe she has gone off somewhere for some special reason. This happens several times. Even we get fed up with our surroundings and are forced to pack up our bags and travel to far-off places, to hills or the seas. This is something like that. Whatever it is, I am sure it is a temporary separation. My heart tells me that she may come back any day.'

So, there are people in the world who have much hope

from animals when I have lost all my faith in mankind. That night, I dreamt of a cat. It was standing atop the chimney of a four-storey government building, looking down on an empty and lifeless city. All the windows and wooden doors of the building had been stolen. It had been several years since smoke had swirled out of its run-down stone chimneys that stood on the rooftop like rectangular pillars, all overgrown with weeds. The next time I saw her again in my dreams, she was in a grassy field, jumping among the bushes in a strange manner, as if trying to grab something from the air. Her jump was so astounding that it looked like some of her screws had come loose. Later, I came to know that cats jump up in the air to try and catch butterflies with their front paws. With the distance between us, it was not possible for me to see the butterflies. That day, it dawned upon me that our dreams accept realities from our wakefulness in the same manner as our wakefulness accepts incidents from our dreams. Although I never mentioned it to the old man, maybe he had divined my interest in his cat. One day, he showed me a framed photograph of Payal, who was standing on an oval table with her front paws latched onto a huge porcelain flower vase, both her triangular ears standing erect. Both her cheeks were swollen in a cheerful grin. The vase, with a bunch of colourful paper flowers sticking out of its spout, stood against a background of a highway with rows of lamp posts in front of a multi-storeyed building. There were silhouettes of people in the windows. It was obvious the photograph had been clicked in a studio with a lot of attention to detail. To be honest, I could not help but admire the artistry that had been applied to the photograph. The photographer was definitely a genius who, by taking the help of a porcelain flower vase and using the backdrop of a glittering highway, had gifted a very ordinary cat a universal appeal. The photograph was in an old album that contained dozens of photographs, all brittle and yellow. The sub-inspector had brought out the album from the pocket of his overcoat, where he kept his torch. He later told me he had been saving the loose-fitting woollen coat with its outdated belt for the final years of his life because he was aware that when a man becomes old, the cold becomes his worst enemy.

'You can guess from this photograph how happy she was with me,' the sub-inspector said. 'She was only two days old when a tomcat attacked her. Her mother drove the cat away, but as the kitten was in a very bad condition, she left her to her fate. She took the rest of her brood with her and went off to some other place. The children in our neighbourhood were having fun with her after tying a rope around her neck when I saved her life. I can assure you she is not an ungrateful animal. I am sure she will return one day. I have strong reasons for saying this.'

I don't know why, but that day, for the first time, I realized how lonely the old man was. So, I decided to help him in the matter. I suggested that we search the locality. The old man couldn't just sit idle and while away his time if the cat was so important to him, especially when I was ready to give him support. This is not a large city. I was sure that if we took a tour along the riverbank, one day, we would find her. He nodded and informed me that he lived in a rented house by the river, which he wanted to buy one day. Unfortunately, when he had given the documents to his lawyer to have a search certificate from the registry office, it turned out there were many claimants to the property. So, he abandoned the idea. 'It's obvious then...' I said to him excitedly, 'Your cat must be somewhere this side of the river. Animals aren't very different from their masters when it comes to these matters. For all practical purposes, they are like us; they don't stray far from their homes. She must have found a new shelter somewhere close to the river unless she has had some kind of an accident.'

'My Payal is alive.' The retired sub-inspector clenched his jaws. It was clear that I had hurt him. Shame coursed through me, and in response his jaws relaxed a bit. He bowed his head and, lowering his voice, said, 'She had come back two days ago, and for several hours, she had taken her seat in her usual corner. She was very hungry. I took care of her and fed her milk. But as I dozed off, she was gone.'

'Is this behaviour not cat-like?!' I looked him in his eyes, overcome with victory.

'Why is it that you always adopt an ethical angle? What are you? A *maulvi*?' He was trying to suppress his anger.

So, he wasn't as stupid as I had thought he was. And with

this, I realized for the first time that although my intention wasn't bad, I had hurt him instead of helping him. To be honest, it wasn't my fault. I remain so caught up in people that I hardly find time to think seriously about animals. And then, what I had said about the cat was not first-hand information. It was based completely on hearsay. And aren't we more vocal and full of confidence when our knowledge is superficial? The truth is, I have never had a dog. The dog in our house isn't some fancy dog, no foreign breed. Out of pity, my housekeeper, Mir, had salvaged it from a filthy sewer. It was very sick then, and his entire body was covered with wounds. I still don't understand what Mir saw in him that not only had he adopted him but had taken good care of him, giving him a new lease of life.

'I am afraid I have hurt you,' I said meekly. 'That wasn't my intention.'

'I don't blame you. As human beings, we never adopt the right attitude towards animals.

'Or it's possible that you have had some bitter experiences with cats?'

'Cats? Is there any person whose path a cat has crossed and nothing untoward has happened to him?' I smiled and tried to lighten his mood. 'Anyway, our house is quite old, and we continuously hear cats mewing in its basement and rooms. In fact, frankly speaking, some of the storage rooms are also delivery rooms for street cats. But they are all stray cats, free and headstrong. They come at their sweet will, break into our rooms and vanish without leaving a trace behind. These cats never cross our paths, except occasionally, when, after a meal, we have a habit of leaving our utensils by the well, where they emerge in cahoots from nowhere to lick them clean. To be honest, I have never seen a cat up close. They just whiz past me. But as people say, cats have nine lives, and all we see through our eyes is only one. Ah! Don't you agree we know so little about cats?'

'I don't know what kind of cats you are talking about. This idea of a cat spelling doom on us by crossing our path is a mere fabrication of our mind. And this whole thing about nine lives is absolute nonsense,' the sub-inspector said, shaking his head in the negative. 'From my experience, I can say that compared to other animals, cats are more at home in the company of human beings. They prefer to live in our shadows because humans and mice have an eternal relationship, and mice are the natural diet of cats. Also, I must admit that the things that you speak about with so much confidence are really mystifying. This is the first time in my life that I have met a person like you.'

'I am not some kind of freak! As a policeman who has seen the world of crime and sin up close, I am sure you have met people stranger than me. And I can say this with full confidence because I have also seen this world of crime and sin very closely.'

'I don't understand.'

'I am a lawyer by profession.'

'Ah, that makes sense!' he said as he shook my hand. His face brightened up, the wrinkles on his cheeks quivering. 'Believe me, I can understand you better now. You guys have that unique habit of playing around with words, and I say that based on my own experience. During my service years, I had to interact with a lot of lawyers. But it is surprising that I never saw you in the court compound. Perhaps there's a huge age gap between us. Or perhaps you deal with civil matters, and as a civil lawyer, you are always drowning in rotten documents.'

No, I tried to correct him. I had been fighting both civil and criminal cases, and in the past twelve years, I had gained quite a notoriety in both. He must have known my father, a famous lawyer in our district. There was a time when his court cases acquired legendary status. But I was still in college when he died, and after him, it was my grandfather who brought me up. He too was a famous barrister of his time, though he had stopped going to court a long time ago. To speak the truth, as a lawyer I had to start everything from scratch, which was better for me. Had I simply inherited a well-established practice, I wouldn't have become what I am today. This is exactly like a banyan tree robbing smaller plants of their natural growth.

'Ah, who doesn't know him? I am sorry to hear that.' His face darkened when he heard my father's name. 'I think he died by suicide, or perhaps someone shot him. I am sorry, I shouldn't have said that so bluntly. You people must have gone through very bad times. It is difficult for a son to face such ordeals; in fact, sometimes, an entire lifetime isn't enough to cope with it.'

Perhaps he was right. But it is also true that, to this day, I haven't been able to understand if my father's death was a tragedy for me or something else.

That day when I returned home and stood in front of my father's photograph, it was impossible for me to understand the psychological reason that had compelled me to reveal so much of myself to the old man. Consequently, our meetings on the riverbank became few and far between. We developed a habit of regarding each other from a comfortable distance. And then donkeys and dogs came between us, and one day, as I stood next to a garbage dump where a bunch of crows were fighting over a dead cat, I forgot him once and for all.

There is a small township across the river where stands a three-storey house on a dirt road. I go to that house to meet Aisha, sometimes on foot and sometimes in a rickshaw. A few years back, Aisha used to be my client. After her husband died, as a lawyer I had helped her in matters of land and inheritance. In addition to her share of the ground floor, she is in unlawful possession of the entire first floor and one half of the second floor of her husband's paternal home, where she lives with her maid and children. The dirt road goes past the cast-iron gate of the house, which is adorned with fishes made of iron that rotate like small bells. It then circles her house and ends up in a field. At some point in the past, marble lions must have stood on both the pillars of the gate. They have vanished now, bushes covering their pedestals. Crusts of dead moss can be seen on the boundary wall, with chameleons lazing around at its top, who, to attract your attention, will immediately assume extremely deep shades. The entire ground floor has been rented out to a baker, one of its doors remaining open towards the road all the time. The baker does not own the place but has been running his business there for such a long time that it has become like his personal property. The rent he owes is very meagre and has become a mere formality, which he now deposits in the rent control office. At Aisha's behest, I have filed many true and false eviction cases against him, but at the same time, I have assured her that she will never be able to take possession of this property in her lifetime because the entire legal machinery of the country has been built in such a way as to give the maximum advantage to a tenant. Half of the second floor and both the rooms on the roof remain locked. Locks of different shapes and sizes hang on other doors as proof that some rooms are still in the possession of Aisha's relatives from her husband's side. Some of them are stamped with government seals.

Whenever I pass by the bakery windows on my way to Aisha's door, a strong aroma of biscuits and cakes freezes my footsteps. I like this aroma. It reminds me of my childhood days when, as opposed to now when biscuits and bread are available even in smaller shops, these things were found only in bakeries. Those days, there was no neighbourhood that would not boast of a bakery or two, where standing in front of glowing chimneys, workers would be seen using iron tongs to push trays of biscuits into or out of the oven. It is because of this aroma that my feet slow down and finally come to a stop in front of an electric pole, which is the last facility pole on that path, throwing its tapered shadow at Aisha's gate. This triple-storeyed house is the last human abode on my path; there are endless rows of grain fields after that. There, in the midst of this cropland, some three furlongs away, is a small village with a clump of palm trees. An old, white church with a tiled roof stands in it. The church, with its tiny towers and minarets, built next to a pond looks like a toy house. Long ago, this village was built by lepers who had been discharged from the missionary hospital, but they dared not to go back to their homes. It is their third generation that is now inhabiting this village. On weekends, the sound of church bells comes to the window, sailing through the fields.

Before I reach her place, which is the only cemented house in the locality, I have to pass through rows of mud huts that are abodes of outcastes. Outside these huts, cows walk around with their brood, their ample udders thrashing across their legs. All the time, they can be seen foraging garbage in the sewerage or mudlarking the toilet pits. Every time I pass through this lane, I am forced to hold a handkerchief to my nose. I wonder what compelled Aisha's father-in-law to build this house here. Perhaps he bought the land dirt cheap, because not only does the house have a huge garden at its back, though this is now in total ruins, but it also has its own private graveyard, where one of the marble lions stands on the grass, gathering dust. With time passing by, it is gradually sinking into the soft soil under the pressure of its own weight.

Aisha would always be the first person to see me before I could spot her. She would send one of her children to guide me home. I like Aisha, and I am of a mind to propose to her someday. But time is passing by, and meanwhile, her elder son has turned fourteen and seems hostile towards me. I mean, he now looked at me like his father would have. I am very close to both her younger sons. Aisha wants me to mingle with her children. She stations herself at the window and busies herself in her embroidery work. While tracing the flower patterns on the fabrics, now and then, she raises her head to cast a cursory glance at the abandoned garden or look across bare fields, where paddy grows in patches while in the sunlight, birds soar in the blue sky. If it is summer and there is a cuckoo call from the palm trees, she yawns and puts down the embroidery work on her lap. It is a green parrot with a red beak. Although once it is completed, there is every probability that it won't look like a parrot perched on a branch with its comb-like leaves but more like a bird soaring through the sky, clutching a piece of a branch. As I pick her handiwork to examine it, Aisha rests her head on the rod of the window, letting out a cold sigh. At this point, her eyes brim over with tears for no apparent reason. I ignore her moist eyes and pay full attention to her younger son's joke. I laugh more loudly than is customary. The house help brings a platter of tea and biscuits as also fried papad and boiled eggs. Often, I am lucky enough to have some special item sent from her father's home. No sooner than I arrive at Aisha's place, her elder son disappears. But I know that he must be somewhere downstairs, roaming outside the bakery or waiting in some invisible corner, impatiently marking time for my departure. On the way back, he follows me, treading on my heels. But I never pay him any attention. My instinct tells me that this is nothing but a sign of a boy growing older.

One day, Aisha raised her head from the frame and looked askance at me. Seeing me distracted elsewhere (although I was attentive towards her), she kept mum for a while, then cracked a smile. 'He smells a rat for no reason.'

I avoid any conversation that involves Nadir, but she keeps staring at me as if she won't let me go without an answer. In the end, I give in.

'There is nothing to be shocked about. He is growing up, and when boys become adults, they take their father's place.'

Aisha puts down her embroidery on an adjacent chair, gets up, and after a deep breath, addresses me directly. 'You mean he is envious of something?' I look at her. Her deep breathing had caused her fair cheeks to flush with blood, and her nose pin glinted in the daylight. She is in a light green Pakistani chiffon suit whose hem reaches down to her ankles.

A muslin dupatta covers her chest, which would slide down at any slight movement, to be pulled up again to its place.

'We should not discuss these things so openly when children are around,' I say, and picking up her wooden embroidery frame, caress the smooth and thick contours of the parrot, made from nylon threads. As I stroke it, I feel a strange sexual desire surge inside me. Aisha's work has a finesse that is usually not to be found in the handiwork of other women nowadays. She goes towards her kitchen, her shapely hips swaying consciously. Whenever I find the opportunity, I undress her in my imagination. Aisha knows my gaze. Perhaps her hips, too, are aware of it. Maybe it is why she always tries to maintain a reasonable distance from me, though I know she does not dislike the way I take an interest in her physique. I have always found her not only well dressed, but she is also done up properly all the time. Not only that, she picks out clothes that scale down her age by a good few years.

When we are alone, I try to hold her hand. She immediately jerks it off.

I look at her with shock. 'Do you want me to stop coming here?'

'Have I ever said that?'

'And you know pretty well why I come here.'

'What do I know?' It was obvious that she was lying.

We fall silent. Then I point towards the river through the open window, though it isn't visible from her house. 'You know pretty well why I care to cross the river on foot and come all the way to your place.'

'It's because it's easy to cross it. Even rickshaws and bullock carts make it through the sand. At least you are a man.'

I take care of Aisha's paperwork. An army of her in-laws are after her. They had even tried to forcefully capture some mango orchards a few miles away. By bringing criminal charges, I had sent some to jail. I was able to have a status quo in Aisha's favour. But this was the professional part of our relationship, and Aisha would always pay my fee without any delay. In some minor cases, she would avail the services of some cheap lawyers without bothering to inform me. She would appear in person in court to take adjournments. She has learnt how to face the police in criminal cases. In those moments, she never forgets to dress up properly, even arming herself with a fancy purse. I am sure that she would not stop short of using her feminine charm if it was of any help in dealing with the court cases or the police.

'Perhaps it is easy to cross this river,' I sigh, 'but harder to go back.'

'You always go back.'

'Do I really go back every time I come to your place? Have I ever really gone back from this place?'

And on the way back in the rickshaw, I notice that her elder son is following me, taking shelter behind electric poles. He follows me all the way to the river, hiding behind bushes that grow along the slope. I don't mind him following me. If I were in his place, I would have done the same thing. The rickshaw stops at a rock by the river. From here, a stony path descends into the riverbed. On the sand stands a roof of country tiles supported by wooden poles. The bootleggers have a flourishing business there. In front of the hut, there are benches for customers – rough wooden planks nailed to crude poles. These planks look useless during the daytime. Occasionally, a dog turns up out of nowhere and rests on them or a lunatic takes a nap there. But as soon as the sun goes down, several dubious-looking people take over the hut. I am sure with the fall of dusk, prostitutes come to this place, their customers in tow. There is a wooden electric pole here whose bulb would be smashed every time it is fixed in its holder.

It is hardly dusk, but the evening is pitch-dark. The rickshaw puller lights up his lantern, and the rickshaw crawls down the stony path into the sand.

No metal was used in the construction of this two-storey brick building. This admixture of lime, stone and brick harks back to the British era, where, except for a few days when the courts were not in session, three generations of our family have been coming, attired in their robes. Between the courthouse and the prison is the prison garden, spanning over one square mile. One can see prisoners in striped overalls – a sign that they are serving life sentences – drawing water from the wells or splitting logs or working in the vegetable patches. Standing on the upper floor of the courthouse, one can see the garden sprawling to its farthest end where, behind the rows of tall trees, stands another two-storey building, which, like the courthouse, has been built with red bricks and mortar, and as per the architectural policy of that time, no iron was used in its construction. Recently, a new boundary wall has been erected around the building. Sentries armed with carbine rifles keep vigil there. Prisoners work in vegetable patches with ropes tied around their waists. The end of the rope is in the hand of a sentry. The bayonets sticking out of their shoulders glint in the sun. The Britishers had built the courthouse because they wanted to use this area, which was devoid of any human population at that time, as a penal colony. But this plan had to be shelved for various unexplainable reasons, and ultimately, this small town turned into a wholesale market for clothes and grains, where merchants would come from far-off places to buy their commodities. But as time passed, the burgeoning population in adjacent districts developed their own trading centres. It's obvious now that this city has lost its significance as the big wholesale market that it once used to be. All along the four sides of this square court building are running verandas, every inch of which is occupied by lawyers, their accountants doing their work on straw mats while typists work furiously on their typewriters kept on small tables. The British built the cast-iron spiral staircases in all four corners of the building, which stand robust and strong even today, whereas the hinges of the wooden staircases, built in independent India, have become worn out and shaky, as if they protest people climbing up or coming down the staircase. The people in nearby streets and markets consider themselves safe from the calamity of nature in view of the lightning conductors that jut out of the roof of the building because, during monsoons, or when storms rage in the sky, grim reports of people dying by lightning come from the surrounding fields. I am a lawyer who wields considerable clout in both criminal and civil cases. Perhaps this is a gift of my genes. Armed with a typewriter, folding chair and wooden table, as also with several bundles of briefs and canvas tote bags cluttered up with files and documents, my scribe and typewriter occupy the southern end of the veranda, spreading a mat thereon (a corner that gets full sunlight in winter, while in summer it has the advantage of being in the shade). This part of the veranda is for our personal use. I reach there only when it is time for the court proceedings to start. The scribe is an employee from my father's time. He is not only very loyal to us but also knows the finer details of each and every case.

Hiranmoy is a Bengali by birth, whom I address as Kaku. He had tried his best to motivate his elder son to become a lawyer, but he joined the Naxalite Movement and was killed in a police encounter. His younger son is mentally unwell and has tried to commit suicide many times. His elder daughter works in a government hospital as an ayah. She is unmarried, and now she is well past marriageable age. His younger daughter has a dubious reputation. But you can't be sure from Hiranmoy Kaku's face that he is depressed on account of these setbacks. Most of his molar teeth have fallen out, and as a result, both his cheeks have sunk in a funny way, and although he keeps his dentures with him, I have never seen him use them. In fact, now we are so used to his partially toothless gums that it does not matter to us. He is a chain smoker, and with a bidi always held between his lips, he remains busy all the time. He minutely studies the papers from behind the blurry lenses of his eyeglasses, or sometimes, taking help from a magnifying glass that he always carries in his pocket. And as I get ready to proceed with the hearing of a case, he will never forget to shoot up from his chair to help me wear my robe.

'Let me be, Kaku.' I try my best to stop him, but this is an old habit of his from my father's time, and no one can rob him of this right.

My hair has been thinning at the forehead. It's the beginning of my hereditary baldness, though, for someone who is just thirty-six, it is too early. However, I can't help it. Baldness is in our family genes, and if I am bold enough to admit it, it is no less helpful in our profession. Inside my chamber, in a wooden frame inlaid with gold, hangs a portrait of my grandfather, a daguerreotype image of his youth in which one can clearly see the individual pixels. Next to it is a portrait of my father, which was taken from a box camera. Both of them grew bald in the same manner, although a hat placed on my grandfather's head saved him from the ignominy of premature baldness. When my grandfather was in his prime, Britishers ruled the country and barristers had to wear this sort of thing. He lived long but lost his memory in his twilight years. In those days, doctors knew very little about this illness. Dad looks much older in his photo, compared to his actual age. When he breathed his last, he was merely fifty-five. I was his only child, born very late to my mother. In his conjugal life, he didn't get along well with my mother.

One day, he fired a gun at his own face, though he wasn't fully successful in his attempt at suicide. He had pushed the trigger holding the butt of the gun between his toes. It was a clumsy effort at death as his thumb slipped, and the muzzle of the gun shifted inside his mouth. Instead of hitting the roof of his mouth, the bullet passed through his nasal cavity, tearing apart his right eye. It shattered the bone in the right side of his forehead. He lived eight more years after this failed attempt, but his condition was worse than a dead man. In those eight years, I always found him lying still on a bed. His face was kept bandaged all the time. He remained insentient till the end of his life. A catheter was inserted into his body through which he passed urine into a pot. After that tragedy struck our house, my grandfather took it upon himself to raise me. Only for my sake, he resumed his practice again, something that he had given up years ago. He started going to the court, but he was a bird of a different clime; the world had changed quite a bit by the time he donned his professional gear for the second time. In fact, newer expedients had gained the upper hand in the corridors of law and justice. He himself was too old to face the new challenges of time and energy. Gradually, he gave up going to the courthouse. His physical condition deteriorated rapidly. This was a time when our house had become a haunt for doctors and nurses. Dad would lie in his room like some wilted vegetable, urine dripping from his catheter while nurses were a harassed lot, tired of cleaning his excreta. I would often watch them behave in a very despicable manner, especially when they thought no one was keeping an eye on them. They would often curse my father, treat him very roughly. In fact, I once saw a nurse lose her temper. She lifted the hem of her sari and urinated on his face, unaware that I was hiding in the room, watching the entire episode from behind a curtain. This incident was so repugnant to me that I couldn't even mention it to anyone. On the other hand, Grandfather would just sit idle and yawn all day or doze off in the shadows of coconut trees, chicklets getting so bold as to come very close to him, pecking at his feet. In his last days, he became very senile. It was the beginning of his dementia. Back then in our town, people didn't know much about this disease. He would often start recalling events of his childhood or youth, stories none of us had ever heard of before. In those moments, he behaved like a child or a young man whose eyes were, for the first time, taking stock of the wonders of the world. It was really surprising to see him so enthused when he divulged the mysterious events of his life, which were otherwise so ordinary. On some days, a nameless mania would take hold of him. He would put his tattered hat on his bald head, a thing that now looked completely ridiculous on his body, and holding on to his walking stick, would set off for some unknown destination. Those were the days when he lost his memory in toto, and gradually, over time, started losing track of time, his present almost gone, while his hazy past would become alive. We tried to make sure that he did not go out, but it was impossible to stop him. He would often forget his way back home or the direction he had taken or even who he was. Once he was found outside a hilly village. He was lying under a tree by the side of a gravelled road, about seven miles away from our city. It was a place he used to go to when he was young, along with his friends, riding their motorcycles. Since he was a known face in the city, some townspeople would always drop him at our gate. Ultimately, I was forced to hang a tablet around his neck, his name, address and telephone number imprinted therein, something that he was not very happy about. I had made the mistake of not making sure that he wasn't aware that I was hanging it around his neck. Once he got the hint, he would throw it off. For a short while, some of my father's juniors handled his briefs. But this was a new crop, very shrewd and impatient to further their careers by hook or by crook, always in a rush to get rich quick. They had sold off their conscience to the devil and behaved like vultures with their clients. They razed the clientele that my grandfather and father had built over the years to the ground. At that time, I was away from home, pursuing my law degree in another city. By the time I finished my studies and returned home to take up practice as a lawyer, most of our loyal clients had gone. Had anyone seen my grandfather of that time when he was counting his days, they wouldn't have believed that this fellow used to be a keen tennis player in his youth. You can surmise that from his photographs hanging from the wall, where my grandpa stands with a British officer in a spotless white tennis uniform, holding a tennis racket in his firm hand. He was such a good tennis player. When I started my law practice, he tried to help me even though he was totally at the mercy of old age. Perhaps he was worried that what with the ambience prevailing in our home, I wouldn't ever manage my career. But he was a lawyer from a different age, and his experience of another era was of no use in our time. As opposed to my grandfather, my father, despite being a successful lawyer, was an introvert, spending most of his time poring over his hardbound law books or guzzling bottles of alcohol. Within two years of my return from law college, my father and grandfather passed away in that order. Twenty-two years have passed since the day my father entered my room completely drunk, but I clearly remember that dragon-like animal. Today, whenever I look at my father's photograph, I see an imprint of that dragon on its glass. A day will come when I will also be no more in this world, and that dragon will be there in my photograph hanging from the wall. As opposed to Dad, Grandfather had a peaceful death, although we can't really call it a peaceful one. It so happened that he disappeared one day from home and remained absent for seven days running. Finally, we found him in a quiet railway station fifty miles from our city. He was lying dead on a bench, hidden among the bushes. The station was in a desolate place, hemmed in by dense forests. He had been hungry for the past whole week, living off drinking water from the only tap that had running water in that station. He had given up the ghost while he was asleep. We wouldn't have found him, but thankfully, he was not aware that the identity tablet was hanging on his neck. I still remember how I wept so copiously for the first time in my life when I reached the platform and saw his lifeless body lying there. It felt like, for the first time in my life, I had been left all alone in the world. We buried him in the public graveyard of our city, next to the grave of my grandmother, who had died within a few years of her marriage. My great-grandfather had bought a large piece of land in the graveyard, and to mark it off from the other graves, we erected a boundary wall around it. Only two months back, Dad had been buried there. For some reason, he had been given a space somewhere in a remote corner, and the bushes and wild plants had swiftly overrun it. Today, only a few of my relatives and acquaintances know of my father's grave. Often, when I would go to the graveyard out of guilt, I would try to trace out his grave among the rotten leaves and grass. It had not only imploded but had been levelled to the ground. So, every time, my search would yield nothing. My grandfather's hookah and gramophone with its brass horn are still in a rake in the company of law books. They are gathering dust there, even though it is a glass bookcase. The chamber is now at my disposal. Grandfather was a die-hard fan of Western classical music, and those records are still stacked carefully in their paper jackets. He was especially fond of Beethoven and had a full collection of his symphonies, quartets and sonatas. One day, I picked up a dust-laden jacket, and out slipped a brand-new record, as if it had never come in contact with a turntable. I tried to play it. But its pin had become rusted, and the sound emanating from the grooves was almost choked. Occasionally, it would explode into a chaotic screech. I couldn't find the box of pins. The only shop in our small town, where one could find a replacement, had now become a cassette outlet, which would blare film songs all day. The owner of the shop told me that the last person who could fix a gramophone had died of tuberculosis. A client of mine advised me to go to Kolkata and check at Wellington Square, where a few gramophone shops were still breathing their last, but by then, my interest in the gramophone had waned. On the other hand, the world had moved on from hookahs. In the distant past, our forefathers must have been landholders. Our old mansion is a reminder of that time, with its human-size windows and rotten beams, which are unable to hold the bricks any more, not to speak of dark, tunnel-like rooms, which have all become so ugly and eerie. I never think of giving a new coat of paint to the walls. I like them as they are. Our last gardener is dead. The garden is now at the mercy of bushes, wild plants and thorny creepers. In the dried flower beds, there are only dead roots or dried stumps, in which snakes slither in full freedom, ferreting around for the rats who breed like hell in the cracks of walls, often emerging from them or the gutters that line the veranda. But apart from the rats scurrying for their dear life, no one pays any attention to them. The snakes, too, return to their pits, which were originally rat holes that they usurped after gobbling up the rats. I once discovered through the curtain of my window a snake who was raising its ominous hood from dried leaves. It had perhaps only just recently discarded its skin because its body was glistening like a newborn babe.

'I just spotted a snake,' I said as I took a puff of my cigarette, lifting my head from the paperwork. Nripen had stopped typing. His feet had gone up in the air.

'Where?'

'It is gone.'

He resumed his typing. Although he was a newcomer, he had already figured out what kind of people lived in the house.

The courtroom of the chief judicial magistrate is overcrowded. A ridiculously large number of bail petitions have come up for hearing. Most of the accused are from remote villages. Their relatives have flocked to the doors of the courtroom; not only the courtroom, but even the veranda is full of people. One can see a sizable number of hapless women in that crowd, all ugly and grim, clutching their babies, breastfeeding them in broad daylight. The children are trying their best to work at the withered nipples. The women have come to see the fate of their husbands, their sole breadwinners.

The Hon'ble Chief Judicial Magistrate is disposing of bail petitions one after another. It is amazing how little time he takes to decide matters so important to human lives. It's my client's turn. The accused is in the cage in the company of other accused. They have unlocked his handcuffs and removed the rope from his waist. The cage is locked from the outside. Cobwebs hang from the ceiling. Both the skylights are besmeared with bird shit. In fact, one skylight still contains a bird's nest whose denizens might have left long ago. There is a film of dust on the wall paint that hasn't been dusted off all these years. The red fabric encasing the wooden banisters and railings is ripped off here and there, thanks to the careless fingers of people who must have unknowingly scraped them off. I look at the accused. He has long, wavy hair that local tribes generally wear, hiding the nape of his neck completely, a pug nose reminding one of the tribal blood he is carrying in his veins. He is a member of a *bhajan mandali*. He is avoiding people's gazes. I must take all measures so that he is acquitted of the heinous charges levelled against him. He has been accused of outraging the modesty of an eight-year-old girl, who nearly died after the incident. The doctors believed her survival was nothing short of a miracle. Unfortunately, in such cases, such miracles go in favour of the accused. She is a dark-complexioned girl with wide eyes. Within the smug ambience of the courtroom, those eyes wear a bewildered look. She is with her father. Demure and self-effacing, both sit at a bench in the last row. She is dressed in a floral frock, her hair gathered at her nape with the help of a cheap plastic hairband. Holding her father's fist tightly with her puny hands, she occasionally hides her face in his lap. At this primary stage, their presence is not mandatory in the court, but the public prosecutor has brought them to impress upon the magistrate the gravity of the case, ensuring that bail is denied to the accused.

Without going into the full details of the case, I present my request for bail in a subdued manner. My client has been charged with a heinous crime. It's obvious that anyone's reaction would be in the negative. But my client is a father, and he has tons of responsibilities on his shoulders. His parents are old, he has a handicapped sister who is a chronic patient of hysteria, suffering from bouts every other day. He has a wife and children. He is the sole breadwinner of his family, and to be honest, he doesn't always get work. So, what does he do for the livelihood of his family? He is compelled to hunt birds with stones and meet his family's needs by selling them. For the last six months that he has been in jail, his family has been on the verge of starvation. If my client doesn't get bail, it will finish his whole family. I am sure that our esteemed public prosecutor will dwell upon potential threats and go so far as to bring charges of bribing when it comes to the matter of bail, which are absolutely baseless in the case of an individual who doesn't even know whether there will be a fire in his hearth the next morning. How can a person who faces starvation on a daily basis and who has the burden of so many people on his shoulders bribe anyone? Is it possible for such people to threaten and scare others? Even if, for the sake of argument, one accepts that such apprehensions are not unlikely, keeping that situation in mind, the court can impose pre-emptive precautionary measures in the form of directing him to present himself every week in the police station or keep a safe distance from the house and relatives of the victim, and so on.

My argument continues for ten minutes. I sketch out his poverty in great detail. This bit about hunting birds with stones is my personal invention. I have used such fictitious incidents in a lot of cases to ensure bail for my clients. I am very familiar with the way life goes on in the countryside. It's an extremely backward region surrounded by rocky hills and infertile plains, where for miles on end, there is an extreme dearth of water. The state government uses this district as a beggar's bowl so that it can get all sorts of monetary help from the central government as also from international welfare organizations. But nobody can say where all this money goes year after year. The district is still in the same shithole it was seventy years back; in fact, it would not be wrong if I say that every year, the situation is going from bad to worse. All the magistrates and judges appointed in the court are outsiders. They have no inkling as to what kind of people they are dealing with. They look at their transfer as a form of punishment, as an exile sentence. I shed some light on delicate nuances in the rape case and cursorily point out a few loopholes here and there, and when I sit down in my chair, wiping sweat from my face with a handkerchief, the junior lawyers, the relatives of the accused, as well as the court staff, all look at me with admiration. Like all places, a booming voice carries its own weight here too. The public prosecutor sat in his chair as if he had nothing to do with the case. The government has fixed his salary. For all practical purposes, he has become an automatic machine. He goes right after me. He carefully organizes his papers in front of him, stands up and adjusts his robe on his shoulders. He takes off his spectacles and studies the case file closely, and after clearing his throat, he starts his one-track argument. If the accused is allowed bail, the child can be threatened and intimidated, and her life will be in danger. The girl's father is a poor farmer. He is a labourer who works in the fields, and with the changing seasons, he is forced to move as well, sometimes spending his days in places hundreds of kilometres away from his home. There is every probability that out of greed, he might put pressure on his daughter to change her statement. The hon'ble magistrate has no interest in the public prosecutor's argument. He is fiddling with one of the paperweights lying on the table.

What the public prosecutor is saying he has heard thousands of times before, and he will probably keep hearing it unless he gets a promotion or is transferred to some other district. On and off, he asks his typist to note down some major points of the case. The court clerk, sitting straight in his chair, stares deeply at the empty witness box. His betel-chewing teeth are the colour of brass. Hc is not allowed to chew betel during the hearing of a case, and he finds it hard to pass the time without it.

The Hon'ble Magistrate postpones his decision until 3 p.m. and retires to his chamber. Perhaps he needs some more time to arrive at a decision. Even in cases much more complicated than this, he does not take much time to decide matters of bail. I step out into the veranda and sit in my folding chair. I refresh myself with a cup of tea. Hiranmoy Kaku is on his floor mat scavenging through some documents. He forwards the deposition of a witness that relates to another case.

'We will have to drum up some witnesses from the defence side,' he says. 'The public prosecutor has lined up his witnesses superbly. We will have to do something to counter it.'

'We will see to that.' I return the document without casting a glance at it. I am not in the mood to go through another case at this stage. That one is a very serious case. The accused are very high profile with a lot of contacts in the corridors of power. No wonder the number of their enemies isn't small. Even a tiny mistake on the part of the defence may throw a noose around their necks. The case is not only political in nature but highly sensitive too. I can't take it lightly.

On the lawn of the court, litigants are crowding around the trees. A madman, dressed in a grimy kurta pyjama, stops in front of a pillar. He has a stick in his hand. He is not very old, but his bushy and grizzly hair has turned grey. I know him from the days of my bar examination when I would come to court with my grandfather. He was a highly educated person who used to give mathematics tuition to school children. Then one fine morning, all of a sudden, he went mad.

This is a very old building with lawns and corridors sprawling all around in such a number that a lot of people can be accommodated in its labyrinth. Dogs and lunatics of the town roam freely among its corridors. This two-storey building, which is three times higher than any normal building, is a haven for lunatics and beggars, who take shelter here from the scorching sun. No wonder all the vagabonds of the world flock to this place. Its high ceilings, thick walls and gothic pillars, not to speak of the wooden staircases, give much-needed relief in summer.

The Hon'ble Magistrate graces the court at 3 p.m.

sharp. He forwards his judgement to the court clerk and casts a glance at the accused, who stands alone in the cage, thrusting his fingers into the wire mesh. He is staring at the trees standing on the lawn. The court clerk stands up, adjusts his spectacles on the bridge of his nose and after clearing his throat, starts reading the last few lines of the verdict written in English. Keeping in mind all the circumstances of the case, as also the gravity of the charges, the court has arrived at a decision that granting bail to the accused will neither serve the purpose of justice nor the law. Hence, the court rejects the bail appeal in its entirety.

This is the second time that the bail petition has been rejected.

The case is adjourned. Tightly roped and properly handcuffed, the accused stands on the veranda. The policemen in charge of him are trying to fleece some money from his relatives, assuring them sincerely that the accused will be treated fairly in jail.

'Don't be scared.' I place my hand on his shoulder. 'I know a senior lawyer in Kolkata High Court. We will file an appeal for your bail there.'

He doesn't say anything. Perhaps he is not interested in any appeal. Maybe, by this time, he has gotten used to the prison. And as he is being led towards the police van under the watchful eye of the constables, I look at the girl from the corner of my eyes. She is with her father. Coming down the steps of the veranda, they are drinking water from a hand pump. Her father, holding the corner of his dhoti in one hand, his umbrella hanging from his back, vigorously works on the lever of the hand pump. The girl is only nine years old, but she has already seen the dark side of the world. In a year or two, she will begin to menstruate, and her life will become darker. Hiranmoy Kaku once again hands me the depositions of witnesses.

'I have underlined the sentences where prosecution witnesses have made mistakes or contradicted one another,' Hiranmoy says. He once again speaks about lining up some defence witnesses without whom we will definitely lose the case. I cast a cursory glance at the documents without touching them and again turn my head to look at the child.

I don't know why, but this girl reminds me of my childhood days.

This happened twenty-two years ago.

It was summer. Armed with slingshots and stones, us friends were roaming outside the Chinese Mansion. Our fight always raged with squirrels, chameleons, moles, dogs, even snakes and mongooses.

'Do you have an idea what the Chinese do with their dead?' Utkal stopped in his tracks with the football ensconced in the crook of his arm. Those were the days when one had to put the rubber bladder separately inside the ball. After the bladder was filled with air, lacing up the muzzle was a herculean task.

Utkal would always come up with such questions in those days. At times, it seemed like the only purpose of his existence was to pose such questions, like Socrates. 'Do they cremate them, bury them or simply feed them to vultures and crows?'

'The Chinese never die,' I replied. 'We live next to the Chinese Mansion, but I have never seen a Chinese funeral. They just get older and older but never die.' Then I remembered the coffin that had been brought out of the Chinese Mansion. 'Perhaps, after getting fed up, their relatives put them in a coffin and leave them in the jungle.'

There was a large drain, whose source was somewhere in the Chinese Mansion. There were clumps of trees that ran parallel to it and opened onto a stretch of barren fields. Here, the forest floor was dank, and being on the outskirts of the city, sanitation workers, taking advantage of the loneliness of the place, would come with their trolleys to dump the carcasses of animals. We would form a picture in our minds of the Chinese dead that roamed about in the forest. Their skins would be so transparent and white that in the sunlight, you could see through them. Since we had been brainwashed from our childhood that the Chinese ate all things that walked or crawled the earth, including snakes and cockroaches, we took it for granted that the spirits of the dead and rotten carcasses of animals would not matter to them.

'Really,' Amjad said, 'I don't think you are wrong. We have seen burning pyres in the cremation grounds. We ourselves bury our dead in graveyards, Parsis feed their corpses to vultures and crows, some people drop their dead into the river. We have read all these things in books. But we have never heard of the Chinese having any cremation ground or graveyard of their own. I am sure some big mystery is involved in this. One day, we should go into the forest behind the Chinese Mansion and explore.'

'People say that the forest is infested with the spirits of the dead Chinese. They come there rowing their boats in the river and get down near the drain.'

'All the more reason that we should go there.'

And although I never really believed that there was a place where the Chinese would leave their dead, I don't know why, but I was deeply convinced of it. Of late, what with these Chinese dead, I have started seeing this part of the city as a very mysterious place. More than 70 per cent of this city's population lives in the older part, where the roads are extremely congested and filthy; at some points, they are merely dingy lanes. Most of its markets are old and dirty, reminding one of the days when this city had been merely a village, but with the arrival of the British, people from far-off places started to converge and settle down here, and thus, by rapidly increasing their number, they had turned it into a town. The other residential parts of the town hark back to a later period when some two-storey buildings had come up. Some havelis had also been constructed, which are now in ruins. A few government buildings are also there, partly in use and partly forsaken. The birds in the trees are the ones that we had seen in our childhood days. But sometimes, we fancy that this city is a weird place, built over a mysterious swampland that always remains buried in a dense fog, which makes it special. And people living here are a mysterious lot, very difficult to understand from the outside. It would not be strange to think someone else lives inside us, peering out through our eyes. The sunlight pours a pale yellow on our tall windows, and the moon descends to our level to shine over our heads.

The summer is here. The criminal case against the rapist is about to start. The public prosecutor has been asked to forward the list of witnesses. The villagers take too long to open up. Most of them don't want to come to court or the police stations, except for a few village idiots or good-for-nothings, who are always ready to go anywhere for a little bit of money. But they get a mere pittance from the allowances they are entitled to as witnesses; a major part of it is usurped by the police constables and court staff. Unlike other times, this time, the public prosecutor appears emotionally involved in the case. After all, the modesty of an eight-year-old child has been outraged, and that too by a forty-year-old man. The hon'ble judge has finalized the charges, and all indications are there that if the accused is convicted, he will receive a life sentence. The public prosecutor has submitted a petition for amendment of the charges so that the charge of death sentence may be annexed. I haven't objected to this. As a defence lawyer, I am going through very tough times. It is not easy to prepare people to depose in favour of the accused. This case pertains to a village where people are fairly conservative. Often, their reactions are collective, and once they adopt a position, you cannot make them budge from it. I told the family members that I intended to go to their village to see the location where the incident took place. But I am hard-pressed for time, and only a few weeks are left before the case will start. In fact, the case can start any day after the summer holidays are over (this summer break is part of a tradition when Britishers were at the helm of the affairs and hon'ble judges used to go off with their entire offices to the hill stations to escape the blistering heat of the plains). The public prosecutor has handed in the list of witnesses who are to be summoned by the court. But it isn't enough to send them summons; the police will have to depute its machinery to bring the witnesses to the courtroom on the hearing day. To make it possible, they are compelled to send uniformed policemen to the village. Once a witness is brought to the witness box and his deposition is recorded, no one bothers whether the witness makes it to his home or not.

'They are again roaming about the mango orchard.' One day, Aisha lands up in my office. Her elder son, Nadir, is with her. He is avoiding my eyes. I look at him with interest, my elbows resting on the table.

'Let them go to hell.' I take out a cigarette from my pack.

'I have sent them to prison once. If they make the mistake of ever setting foot in the orchard, they will rot in prison, and this time, it will be very hard for them to get bail. You have been making rounds of the court for such a long time. You must know what "status quo" means. Rest assured the orchard will remain in your custody until the case is decided. If anything goes wrong, I am here to help you. By the way, it's mango season already.' I fake an interest in the matter. 'I have never had a chance to visit your orchard.'

'Name any day you like.' Aisha is evading my gaze. 'There are other trees also in the orchard, apart from mango. There is a rest house with two rooms. Sometimes, we go there and stay for a few days. It was a favourite spot of Nadir's grandfather. After completing Hajj, he would spend most of his time there; in fact, he took his last breath there. I can get it cleaned up for you if you want to go there.'

'Really?' I sit up straight in my chair. 'I had no idea that such an arrangement is possible.' The boy meets my gaze for the first time.

'Don't you go to school?' I ask him. The boy remains silent.

'He has his final school exam this March.' Aisha grasps her purse and stands up. She sighs and wipes the corners of her eyes with a handkerchief. 'People won't let a widow live in peace.'

After they are gone, I bring the mango orchard to my imagination in all its splendour. It is so vivid as if I were there.

I have been dreaming of the orchard. A woman lives in a villa there. Her nipples are lilac. She is always seen sitting nude by one of its windows. Holding a fancy comb in her hand, she keeps tidying up her hair that falls down to her ample buttocks. This woman is Aisha. Over the treetops, wild ducks sail across a blue sky. I always see migratory birds in my dreams, and they always cross a blue sky, and they would always be wild ducks. As a matter of fact, what with the distance between us, they always look like wild ducks to me. The earth below is covered with a riot of purple flowers. These may be paper flowers for all I care. The person guarding this orchard is an old geezer, but he is adept at keeping the secrets of an illegitimate intimacy to himself, keeping them locked up in his heart. He kneels before me and welcomes me by throwing some flowers in front of me. Aisha is walking around under the trees. Both of us are naked. Our private parts are covered with pubic hair.

'Who gave you the address of my secret garden?' Aisha repeats her question over and over again.

'It was you,' I answer.

It is summer vacation in the court. One day, I set out for the rapist's village. Hiranmoy Kaku is with me. There is a charred sun in the sky. We get off a bus and cover a long distance on foot, holding an umbrella over our heads until we reach a plain from where the village comes into view. It is surrounded by palm trees. Eagles and crows are circling in the sky. At the end of the treeless plain sits the rapist's father in the sparse shade of a tree, the rows of croplands forming his background. He is waiting for us with an umbrella. He stands up and receives us with a namaskar. He guides us to his village, leading on the ridges of cropland. On the way, there are clumps of *shimul* and *palash* trees, where jackals howl on winter nights. Most of the houses have tin roofs, and almost every courtyard has a neem or *peepal* tree casting its shadows on the ground, but the tree that is ubiquitous in every courtyard is the drumstick tree. This is because not only does this plant grow fast, but it is also an opulent source of vegetables for poor villagers. Some way off from the village, there is a government-owned well, which has dried out completely. A narrow path leads to the cremation ground by the river. At one end of the village, there is a government primary school whose tin roof has collapsed. Undaunted by the scorching sun, a black-faced monkey sits atop the wall, staring at us. Maybe he is surprised to see us materialize from nowhere in such blistering heat. His long tail hangs down from the wall. His presence indicates that a whole bunch of monkeys is somewhere nearby. The school building is no longer in use. Now the school children have only the open sky over their heads. Anyway, schools in villages remain closed in summer and the rainy season.

We are very thirsty. Hiding her face in a long veil, the rapist's wife offers us water in heavy brass glasses. With the intensity of the heat pressing on our bladders, we like the taste of cool water, though the glass is very heavy and it is a bit difficult to drink in one go; there must be a significant quantity of iron in it. The rapist's father sits down on his charpoy. His knitted eyebrows are shaggy and white, reminding us of a special breed of dog. In the shadow of a wall, a few emaciated goats are taking rest, chewing cud.

'The villagers don't talk to us since this happened,' he tells us. Though his accent is pure Bihari, one can clearly observe an undertone of Bengali, typical of this place.

'That's natural,' I say. I am adept in all sorts of tongues native people use as I have been handling rural cases for so many years. 'You can't expect them to laud you for such things.'

The old man keeps silent. The woman begins to sob into her veil. This is the wife of the rapist by second marriage. It has been two years since his first wife died. He has several children from his first wife, none of whom I see right now.

'Take me to the crime scene,' I say, fed up with the whole ambience. I don't like this village. It feels so lonely here.

There is absolute silence on the village path. As we pass through its small market, we notice that the shutters of all the shops are down. Not a soul is visible anywhere. Surely this isn't on account of the scorching heat. Maybe the villagers received the news of our arrival, and they didn't want to be a part of it. There is a jujube orchard some way off from the village, across a rain-fed drain. The drain is dotted with large pieces of rocks. In fact, at some points, it's difficult to tell if we are walking in a drain or moving among the rocks. All the way to the orchard, rows of date palms sway in the wind, most of them rotten to the roots, though bunches of dates hang stiff from their trunks. The orchard, built on a rise, has a decrepit boundary wall of mud, which, facing rain and storm over the years, has melted down at some places to its base. Its gate is made of gnarled branches of jujube trees, reinforced by discarded electric wires. The old man opens the gate, and we enter. This is a lopsided gate, sagging precariously at one end. It looks like the gate is opened and closed endlessly and has created a kind of circle in front of it with human footprints.

'So. This is your garden?'

'Yes, sarkar.'

This isn't the season of berries. The trees give way to a clearing strewn with dust and stone. There are also a few mango trees in the orchard, but there is no sign of fruits on them. To my surprise, I find a ripe mango lying on the ground. I pick it up. It is warm, and baked by the intense heat, it has become flaccid. I examine it closely and bring it up to my nose. Its aroma reminds me of my bitter childhood. I throw away the mango and rub my hands together to get rid of its smell. Encrusted with lac insects, the thorny jujube branches remind me of elephantiasis.

'This is the place where, according to Mahua's family, Lalan brought shame on her.'

The old man points to a corner where misshapen rocks have broken through the land. The boundary wall there is overrun with thorny bushes. 'They showed this spot to the police.'

'Did the child accompany them?'

'No, sarkar. We came to know that the police were eager to bring her here, but Mahua had caused a lot of commotion.'

'All the better. By the way, what do you think? Do you think they have made it a bigger deal than it is?'

'Absolutely, sarkar. What would have Lalan seen in that girl? This is all about a land that emerged from the river.'

'Land emerging from the river?'

'Yes, sarkar.' The old man sways on his walking stick. His moustache hangs from his nostrils like a squirrel's tail. 'The land had risen at a place where the river changed its direction. They staked a claim on the land when the land adjacent to our own land had fallen to our lot. Who would be interested in such a fallow land that was completely buried in sand? We had been reclaiming that land for a long time. The problem started when they found that we were growing vegetables there.'

'So, Lalan is completely innocent?'

'A hundred per cent. We are brahmins by birth. I swear by my *janeu*.'

I study the old man. He looks ignorant, but he is not stupid. Rather, he is a very smart person. They aren't as poor as I had tried to establish in the court at the time of the bail hearing. Rather, it's the opposite. But what has that got to do with me? No matter what, I can't help but fulfil my role as a defence lawyer.

'Boys and girls from other villages must be coming to this orchard to steal berries.'

'Who doesn't, sarkar? Every other day, Lalan would have a fight with the villagers. We try to resolve the fight. Children are children; when berries are ripe you can't stop them. But who can explain it to Lalan? He is so hot-headed.'

'And they are of a habit of trespassing by scaling the wall or the gate?'

'Absolutely, sarkar; you said it before I could.'

'Arrange some witnesses from the village,' Hiranmoy intervenes. He has understood my clue.

'Who do you think will testify on our behalf? We have a handful of relatives. They, too, live in a village across the Golad drain. The rest of the villagers are lower caste Rajwars or Bauris or tribal farmers. Landless people as they are, come monsoon, they will leave for Damodar Valley.'

'We will masquerade their relatives as villagers,' Hiranmoy whispers in my ears.

'There is no other way,' I agree.

We return to the village. The old man brings some jaggery on a brass plate, but we avoid partaking of it. We drink tea, which has a strange brackish flavour, as if someone had dissolved copper in it. We leave more than half of the tea in their bowls. We don't stay long in the village. On our way back, Kaku is grumbling loudly.

'What is it, Kaku?'

'Nothing,' he says. But I know what he hasn't said. He is fully convinced that the rapist took advantage of the loneliness of the orchard and committed this despicable act out of spite. It is probable that he did it in a fit of rage, just to take revenge. But Hiranmoy is a professional, and it doesn't take him long to control his emotions.

'You are on the right track,' he tells me. 'We will have to ascertain from the doctor's report in which direction we should steer our case.'

'I have seen that report. A girl at such a tender age cannot be forcibly raped without vitally injuring her private parts. It's true that the girl had to stay in the hospital for a month, but all the wounds are external. The rapist failed to penetrate her. He had tried to force himself in but ended up injuring the girl superficially; all the wounds are confined to the clitoris and the labia majora. The doctor's report is completely silent on the presence of any lacerating wounds on the uterus. It seems that he ejaculated outside. This report was the clumsy handiwork of a physician on the payroll of the government; you can't make these dumb asses do their job spot-on.'

The dogs were making loud noises outside the Chinese Mansion. How old was I then? A mere fourteen-year-old boy and all I think now is that dogs who do not have any masters have every right to bark at their sweet will. Sitting alone in my chamber, the same thought returns to me time and again – that one fine morning I am going to enter the Chinese Mansion to solve its mystery once and for all. But I don't know what the mystery is that I am so obsessed with, or is there any mystery at all in it, or is it a mere speculation on my part that has taken hold of my mind? The Chinese Mansion – I have never seen a human being come out of its door or peep out from any window, except for a hand or two that will dangle out to pull the window shut, or a face or two, which would immediately turn into a profile, leaving its dim outline in the air. But right now, the rapist's case has occupied me completely, and I don't know why I feel like I have already started losing the case, for which my conscience is to be blamed. Whatever the circumstances, a defence lawyer has no right to grab the chair of a judge. But truth be told, the actual nuances of a case start to reveal themselves once the case starts in full swing, although some features of the defence also emerge with them.

Surrounded by relatives of the accused, I sit in my veranda, listening to their jabber. Kaku is not interested in them. He is deeply engrossed in some other documents. The father of the rapist has sold off a piece of his land. He generously pays my fee. I pull a cigarette out of my packet and light it with a matchstick. I shake the matchstick to extinguish the flame.

'You will get a list of government witnesses from Kaku,' I say to the father, letting out a stream of smoke from my nostrils. 'See what you can do about them. It will be very helpful if you break one or two of them. By the by, you must work out some witnesses of your own.'

'Don't expect anything good from these illiterate people.' Kaku raises his head and shakes it in the negative. 'I have to do something about it. We have no alternative but to bolster the defence with our own witnesses. These villagers are inveterate liars. The moment they come in front of a judge, their minds go blank.'

The Chinese Mansion... As I sit on my veranda, I think deeply... Dogs without masters have every right to bark in whichever way they want. A snake slithers past my shadow. Or perhaps it's my imagination. The snake is a strange creature. In this country, we have never accepted them as our own; we never stop short of killing them the moment we catch sight of one, as if this is our divine mission, despite the fact that Hindus worship them as an incarnation of God. On the contrary, thousands of miles from here, in China, this very cursed entity grows wings and takes the form of a dragon, a mythological animal, which even today, is a symbol of fertility, happiness and eternal life, whose photos Chinese people hang on the walls and doors of their homesteads to ward off evil spirits, and these are the very dragons that over and over again appear before me in the sky. The first time I saw it, my father had shot himself in the face. Seen in this context, it's nothing more than a bad omen for me. But a good amount of time has since elapsed – thirteen or fourteen years at the minimum – from when I last saw it. Perhaps my vulnerable mind as a child had tricked me into believing in it. I look at our garden, which has become dark. What must Kaku's debauched daughter be doing right now? Sitting at my table in the chamber, I prepare my first drink. My forefathers are staring indignantly at me from their golden frames. It doesn't matter how terribly immoral or wicked they had been, they would always want their progenies to take the right path. Or perhaps it's not their fault. Perhaps the photographers, as per their habit in the old days, taking the help of colour pencils and brushes, had made them too stern. *Okay, that's enough!* I look back at the photographs with annoyance.

The rapist's case has taken a curious turn. Suddenly, the hon'ble sessions judge has developed a keen interest in it. When the nine-year-old girl is brought into the witness box, he looks at her in utter surprise. He can't believe that someone could look at a girl so wafer-thin from a sexual point of view. This entire case is unbelievable to him. He has made some changes to the charge sheet. He has also had a conversation with the child, all alone, in his chamber. He is a quiet man, of average height. No one has ever seen him smiling in the court. I really respect this sessions judge. At the district level, he is the brightest star in the firmament of justice.

When the child is brought to the witness box to depose under oath, the courtroom is packed with onlookers. At the judge's order, except the lawyer, public prosecutor, court clerk, typist (whose typing machine is placed on the judge's table at his right end), the orderlies, the girl's father, a few relatives of the accused and the constables guarding the accused, everyone else is ordered out. But some people sneak back by the time the case starts. Although this decision to ask people to leave the court is against the principles of justice as a trial is supposed to take place in open court, both the public prosecutor and I, too, do not see anything wrong with it. After all, the case relates to a nine-year-old child who was brutally raped a year ago. The proceedings hardly start when a few policemen pull back the curtain and occupy the last benches of the courtroom. The hon'ble judge doesn't pay any attention to them. It is impossible for him to keep watch on every minor detail. And anyway, there seems to be a permanent night in the judge's courtroom where things are only partly visible all the time. In the entire building, the courtroom allotted to the sessions judge is quite big, proportionate to his rank, and its curtains remain always drawn, especially in summer. All the lights of the courtroom are switched on, including the lamps on the judge's table, once the court is in session. The sessions judge likes to keep his courtroom partly dark. Maybe his eyes are intolerant to bright daylight. Come summer and people are really relieved by this arrangement. Everywhere, from the ceiling to the walls of the courtroom, long iron pipes hold outmoded electric fans that rotate continuously with their pot-like bases. What with the perpetual darkness reigning in the court (no one bothers to dust off the dust and cobwebs from the light bulbs and tube lights), no sooner the case starts than an eerie silence prevails, lending the ambience a dreadful air. Even while the proceedings of the court are on, one can see one or two sparrows perched atop the canopy of ceiling fans.

At times, when pin-drop silence prevails in the courtroom, their chirping shatters it. All the wooden fences and railings are draped in red cloth. Though the benches, tables and chairs are made of very expensive wood, the mesh wires of the prisoners' cage are all rusted and warped at the corners. The floor of the cage is grimy, though its floor is swept every day. The door of the judge's chamber opens onto the rostrum. All he is required to do is take three steps upward, and he will be at the rostrum, where his straight-backed chair awaits him. A heavy curtain always hangs at his chamber door. No one can enter it, except the orderlies, court officials or stenographers.

The girl, all alone in the witness box, looks very nervous. She is so frightened that she fails to even recall her name when it is asked by the public prosecutor. Ultimately, the hon'ble judge has to intervene. He tells the girl her name and asks her to corroborate it. The girl suddenly remembers her name and nods. The name is dictated by the hon'ble judge, which the typist types on his machine promptly. The hon'ble judge gestures to the public prosecutor to carry on with the proceedings. The girl haltingly recounts the whole incident in response to the public prosecutor's mild interrogation; she was picking jujube in the orchard when the accused came up from behind and forced himself on her in a corner of the garden. The hon'ble judge translates every sentence into English, which is immediately typed out. The public prosecutor asks his final question.

'Can you identify the man?'

After being asked the question over and over again, the girl finally understands it. She turns back and casts a timid look at the accused, who is standing alone in the cage. She nods. The public prosecutor breathes a deep sigh of relief.

It's my turn now. In cases like these, the most unpleasant task falls to the lot of a defence lawyer. He is compelled to make the key witness confront such questions that could paralyse his or her tongue, and this is exactly what I do.

'So you sneaked into the garden to steal jujube? You have confessed to this.' The child remains mum. This isn't what they call stealing in the village!

She finally nods after I repeat my question time and again.

'And you very often go into the orchard to steal berries?' The child remains silent. No bird chirps on the fan's canopy. 'He must have caught you in the act many times before?'

She bows her head and agrees. She had been thwacked several times for this, she admits.

'And you still had the courage to go inside the garden?'

'That isn't a question,' the hon'ble judge intervenes. Due to the light coming from the table lamps, his hands are more perceptible than his face. 'The defence lawyer should keep in mind the age of the child. Questions shouldn't be asked to stupefy her. And they should relate to the core of the case itself, especially to the events of that day. And what's your intention in repeating the same question so many times?'

'I seek the forgiveness of the court,' I say. Placing my hands on the table, I bend in reverence. 'Keeping in mind the girl's tender age, I will try to finish my examination as briefly as possible. I take back what I have said.'

'You said that when he caught hold of you, he took you to a corner and forced himself on you?' I throw my next question at the girl.

The child tries to make sense of my interrogation.

'What do you mean by forcing himself on you?' I knew it wouldn't be easy for a nine-year-old to answer the question. 'Okay, tell me, what were you wearing at the time?' I go on.

The girl mumbles the word 'frock', casting a fearful glance at her father, who is sitting on a bench with his head bent low. His gaunt shoulders are as high as his ears. Despite the tube lights installed on all the walls throwing enough life on his head, his hair looks lustreless.

'Only frock?'

The girl looks at me with panic, as if she had not expected such a question from me. I feel pity for her and soften up a little. I say, 'When he caught hold of you, what were you wearing under the frock?'

'Objection, my lord!' The public prosecutor jumps up from his chair. 'The child's age should be considered before asking such questions.'

'Objection overruled,' the Hon'ble Judge says immediately. He is rubbing his hands in regret. I have hit the nail right on its head. 'The defence lawyer's question is well within the purview of the law. It doesn't include any suggestion. The court cannot stop a defence lawyer from asking these questions.'

'Right. You have not yet told us what you were wearing apart from the frock.'

'Tell us, child.' The judge leans forward on his table, looking affectionately at the girl. He has removed his glasses to allay the girl's fear and is looking at her very kindly.

'Don't feel shy. You will have to answer this question.'

'Your Honour, I take back my question,' I say and again address the child. 'What did he do after he caught you?'

'He forced me on the ground.'

'Then?'

'Then...' Her eyes are brimming over with tears.

'Yes, then?' I say, making my tone a little harsh. 'Tell us. Tell us what happened after that.'

The child looks at her father in utter helplessness. Resting his chin on the bent handle of his umbrella that he holds between his legs, he is staring down at the checkerboard floor as if he can vanish into it any minute.

'Tell us, what did he do after he took you to the corner?' The judge intervenes. Perhaps his quiescent asthma has woken up.

'He... my underwear...' The tears roll down her cheeks. She finally lets loose a scream and starts crying loudly.

The court is adjourned for a while. When the court reconvenes and the esteemed hon'ble judge graces his chair once again, I start my interrogation exactly from where I had left it. The girl looks less nervous this time.

'I remember you were trying to say that he took off your

underwear,' I say. And although I am unconsciously leading the witness with that question, the public prosecutor makes no objection to it as, according to his view, this question doesn't weaken his case in anyway.

The girl nods. The lower jaw of the courtroom clerk drops open. He is looking at the girl lecherously, as if she is being raped right in front of his eyes.

'Then what did he do?'

'He... he...'

The girl is completely flustered.

'What did he do with you?' I say with irritation.

'Come on, tell us clearly. Don't be scared,' the judge intervenes again. 'Say everything out loud in the court. This is very important, child.'

'He... took me...' She can't say anything further. And after that, even to minor questions, she doesn't open her mouth. The prosecutor looks crestfallen. He has no other eyewitness apart from her.

'Your Honour...' He stands up and fixes his robe on his shoulder, which is hanging on his back askew as he had been sitting on it all the time. In the mercury light, his robe has assumed a glint as if it were the skin of a freshly polished shoe. 'There is no need for so much interrogation. She is just a nine-year-old child who has grown up in a village. Whatever she has said so far has made all the things quite clear. If we repeat that scene over and over again, it can have a very bad effect on her nerves.'

'I regret it.' The esteemed hon'ble judge once again rubs his hands regretfully. I have realized that the judge's hands are more vocal than his face. 'I can't stop the defence lawyer from cross-examining the witness. These unpleasant questions are bound to crop up in a rape case.'

'So tell us, what did he do with you? He made you lie down on the ground, he pulled down your underwear, and then what did he do?' My booming voice echoes in the courtroom.

My last words are drowned in a loud male shriek. After taking a jump from his bench, the child's father heads towards me, waving his umbrella above his head, when he bangs his leg on the corner of a bench and falls flat on his face. He tries to stand up when the police constables jump over him. He shouts loudly, uttering ineligible words while copious tears flow down his cheeks. On the other hand, sitting on the floor of the witness box with knees drawn to her chest, the girl wails inconsolably, hiding her face behind her palms. Slumped on his chair, the hon'ble judge holds his forehead in his hands. It looks like the hands that are holding his forehead aren't the same that usually move about in the lamplight.

'Amazing! That was great.' Kaku folds my uniform, looking affectionately at me. 'You were unbelievable. All we need now is to deal with the doctor. I have come to know that the new doctor is someone we can buy easily. He is an absolute idiot, a lower caste who has become a doctor through reservation.'

I don't like Kaku's mode of thinking. But what can one do with a man who has been defeated on every front of life? He has only his caste that he can boast of and carry as a consolation prize.

As a result of the unpleasant incident that took place in the court, I am not feeling well. On my way back, it dawns on me what a curse my profession has become. I set out on foot towards the Chinese Mansion. Walking in a leisurely way, I keep an eye on the slanting shadows that the walls are throwing on the road while the sun is gradually going down, and though there is still daylight in the sky, I perceive a light on the first floor of the Chinese Mansion. Some pedestrians pass by me, talking in very loud voices when they had no need to do that. I enter my house. Kaku is in conversation with a client. Maybe some other case is being taken care of. Both are whispering in each other's ear as if two criminals are making some plan to commit a crime. At one point, both of them look up at me but don't say anything. A copy of the doctor's report is on the table. I take it up and cast a glance at it.

'The report can go in anyone's favour,' Kaku looks up and says. 'You will have to work hard on the doctor. I think you can do that.'

'Have we established contact with him?'

'Leave that to me.'

'No, the doctor's testimony is very crucial to the case,' I say. 'I want to meet him personally.'

The public prosecutor has only a few witnesses. After the deposition of the child, his most vital witness is the doctor who had examined the child after her alleged rape. The public prosecutor is working very hard on the case, but it doesn't take me long to demolish him completely. No one saw the act being committed. The girl hasn't been able to divulge enough details during examination or cross-examination to implicate the accused. Since it was a desolate winter afternoon, no one saw the girl enter the jujube orchard or come out of it. There is no other eyewitness except the victim herself. The few witnesses lined up by the police turn out to be mere circumstantial witnesses yielding some far-fetched conjectures. They do not serve the public prosecutor in any useful manner. We also established contact with the doctor who had examined the child and compiled the medical report regarding the state of her private parts. It turns out that he can be easily bought off. A few pegs of hard drink, and he starts ranting about his wife's cruelty.

'I had never hated her as much as I do now.' Under the influence of liquor, his eyelids narrow down to slits. 'But sooner or later, a man sees things as they are.'

I am ashamed of this good-for-nothing medico. He pushes the wads of notes into his briefcase without any loss of face.

On the third day of the court proceedings, as the public prosecutor sits completely confident after examining his witness, it is time for me to chip away at his confidence.

'So you say that there are severe wounds on the girl's

private parts?' I knowingly place my hand on the railing of the witness box in between his hands. This was a trick to establish physical contact that we lawyers use with the witnesses of our rivals, especially with witnesses who seem pliable to us. And in the present case, this witness is on our payroll.

'Yes, this has been laid down in clear terms in my medical report. I have been saying exactly the same thing all along. How many times should I repeat it? Everyone should understand it by now. I have recorded everything in detail in my forensic report. I can only tell you the entire situation after going through my report again.'

'Here is a copy of your report.' I try to hand over a copy. I am trying to read his face. I have a foreboding that this isn't the same man that I met two days ago.

'The wounds are easily visible on the exterior part of her body. The labia majora, the outer folds of her private parts, and the clitoris have been badly lacerated, and it's evident that there has been an attempt to insert something harsh using an unnatural force.' He reads out from the copy of the medical report forwarded by the public prosecutor and looks up at me. He has not accepted my copy.

'But you haven't mentioned the forceful penetration of any male sex organ into the small uterus.'

'We must not have found signs of lacerations there. It doesn't mean that a sexual organ wasn't inserted inside. Some uteruses have enough elasticity to withstand the worst kinds of penetration.'

'But the small uterus of a child at this age remains unformed, and it's only natural for it to be lacerated easily if it encounters any hard object; in fact, it's inevitable. I have even heard that girls lose their capacity to bear children once and for all after they encounter such incidents. But your report doesn't shed light on any of these aspects.'

'I am not denying that, but as I have said earlier, we must not have found signs of laceration there, which is why I haven't written down anything about it. Sometimes, the male sex organ cannot reach all the way up to the small uterus, even where there is an incident of forced coitus; at other times, it is not strong enough. Also, a lot of things depend on the shape of the male sexual organ. And I would also like to add that, sometimes, such things are offset by premature ejaculation. But looking at how clearly the labia majora and clitoris have been ruptured, we cannot deny that there was an attempt of forceful insertion by some hard object.'

The public prosecutor is all smiles. If you believe him, I have been caught in my own net. 'And what can that object be?'

'What can that object be?' The doctor raises his head from the report and looks at me in confusion.

'That's the thing that I am asking from you. What can it be?'

'What can it be?' The doctor looks up at the hon'ble judge. There is a befuddled look in his eyes, as if he expects some kind of help from him. The doctor's glasses glint in the mercury light. He has a habit of squinting in stressful situations. 'A hard and sharp object, if I may venture to suggest?'

I can see that he is breathing heavily. This may be the result of my standing very close to him. Perhaps he has suddenly remembered the wads of cash that he had pushed into his briefcase. 'For example, if someone uses his male reproductive organ with all possible strength?' I ask.

'It's possible.'

'Or a piece of wood or iron or a sharp, pointy object like stone?'

'Maybe. I can't say anything with certainty.'

'There is a mention of a possible male reproductive organ in your report, but it has been dealt with as a conjecture. Even if it is accepted, is it possible that a human reproductive organ, for example, that of a man forty years old, would have so much hardness and sharpness as to cause such "lacerated" wounds or rupture as you say?'

'It's possible.' He nods timidly, his voice becoming very low. It's obvious from the comportment of the hon'ble judge that he has lost all his faith in the doctor.

'In such a situation, there definitely would be wounds on the reproductive organ of the accused, too, but your report is completely silent on this aspect, whereas, so far as I have been able to know from the hospital register, you had examined the accused too.'

The doctor is scratching his head. He looks at the public prosecutor but gets no help from him.

'If I say that in all likelihood, these wounds were caused by a sharp piece of wood or a sharp stone, what would you say to that?'

'I object, Your Honour!' The public prosecutor stands up. 'The defence lawyer is trying to lead the government witness.'

'Objection sustained. Defence lawyer, please try and present your argument in the form of questions only.'

'Actually, this is my question, Your Honour. And my question is very simple and straightforward. Can we expect such toughness from a male sex organ as to cause such a severe wound?'

'I beg your pardon!' The doctor is losing his grip on his case. He is bent so low over the wooden rail that his cheeks are flushed. 'What are you driving at?'

'If I say that this wound was caused by a sharp piece of wood or a pointy stone, for example from a knotted branch or from a piece of flint that can be found in mud walls in villages, what is your opinion about that?'

The doctor looks at me without blinking his eyes. He turns his face towards the hon'ble judge and scratches his head. 'It's possible.' He looks at the public prosecutor. There is apprehension in his eyes. 'In fact, this is more likely.'

Money has done its job. Or perhaps unaware, I have unlocked the door of truth.

The hon'ble judge gapes at the doctor with open contempt. He takes a deep breath and sits up straight, aligning himself completely with the back of his chair. The public prosecutor immediately declares the doctor hostile and cross-examines him. But this time, the doctor doesn't have anything more to add.

The examination and cross-examination of witnesses on both sides are over. Any day, arguments may start. But before that, we will have to take copies of depositions and figure out the nitty-gritties of the case. On my part, I will have to do a lot of things. Meanwhile, the dogs in the backyard of the Chinese Mansion have been causing a lot of ruckus. In reaction to their barking, Jhabra has been behaving in a wild manner. Mir takes him outside. He sometimes lets him mingle with the stray dogs so that he can satisfy his natural urges. I hear his lustful bark from outside the boundary walls of my house, an animal completely triumphed over by sexual desire, making a pitch for a bitch or a dog. That reminds me of Aisha. Aisha, who has started casting deep shadows over my desire, just like the Chinese Mansion. Often, after I am very tired of routine work, I close my eyes and strip off her clothes. Aisha has become a very useful tool for masturbation.

The public prosecutor's argument moves along predictable lines, turning more into an entreaty than an argument, where the story of outraging the modesty of a child is repeated several times over, as if this sentence by itself is enough to tighten the noose around the neck of the accused. According to him, the whole idea of justice would be aborted if it does not go in that one direction. The esteemed hon'ble judge had anticipated a bit more acumen from him. He is totally disappointed in his argument. He loses interest in him right in the middle of it and looks sideways, taking a glimpse of the veranda ceiling through the oval skylight. The skylight contains a small hole for ropes to pass through so that the hand-pulled fans can be operated from outside. These small holes, now useless, have become mere entryways for the birds, the walls around the hole besmeared with bird shit. I realize that he is simply waiting for the public prosecutor to wrap up his argument so that I can start my disputation. I have lined up a few witnesses from the side of the defence in a bid to cook up a fake story of a family feud. I had avoided the whole issue of 'dry riverbed' that had emerged from the river, except for a casual reference to it at some point of argument because there is a complete absence of paperwork about it. The public prosecutor tries very hard to expose the lies of these witnesses, but he utterly fails in the course of cross-examination. He had felt no need to go to the village. There is a cultural barrier for him that he declines to cross. He hates the way the villagers distort his mother tongue, Bengali. He has a mania for Rabindra Sangeet, and if required, he can even sing a few songs on stage. However, his love for Bengali culture is narrowed down to that imagined circle that has not been drawn by the poet Tagore. If you believe him, only barbarians dwell outside that imagined circle.

When I commence my argument, the courtroom is overcrowded with lawyers, policemen and people who had come to attend other cases but have assembled out of curiosity. A deep silence descends in the courtroom, and although I am presenting my argument in English, people are all ears to what I am saying as if they understand each and every word.

I begin my argument by probing gaps in the statements of prosecution witnesses where they have cancelled out one another (and this takes up a lot of my time). Finally, I arrive at the events of the day when the crime was committed. 'Your Honour, I will never go so far as to say that the child has made a false accusation in the courtroom. It's probable that the accused, in a fit of anger, had hit her, like he had been doing in the past, which people now see as rape. The defence has also presented a few witnesses who have informed us that for a long time, a feud has been going on between the two families over some land. But this dispute apart, what I clearly understand is that, and for this, I would like to draw your attention to that part of the testimony of the public prosecutor's Witness No. 4 where he has confirmed during cross-examination that the orchard's gate was built by assembling the knotted branches of a jujube tree, and if a person isn't careful enough while crossing over it, it is natural that his crotch will be injured. On the other hand, if we believe the government doctor, it is more probable that the injury might have been caused by a thorny branch of the jujube tree with which people are of a habit of building their orchard gates because, what with their thorny nature, it is very difficult to trespass through such gates. The doctor has clearly said that one cannot expect such toughness from a human organ as to ensure such a severe wound. Moreover, the accused, as Your Honour yourself can see, is at such an age, given that he is a married man, when it is not possible for a human being to be capable of such toughness.'

'What are you trying to imply? Do you mean that the accused is impotent?' The judge looks at me sarcastically. His hands are completely still on the table under the lampshade.

'Absolutely, Your Honour. You guessed what I had been driving at for so long. And since you have pointed in that direction, I would like to present a medical certificate that will substantiate my point.' I forward a doctor's report to the court clerk. 'The wife of the accused died a year ago, after which he is in such a severe shock that he has lost his potency.'

'This is preposterous.' The public prosecutor jumps up from his chair to protest vehemently. 'We have no knowledge of any such report, nor have we been given a copy of it.'

'The government cannot allow a new witness at this point. It's too late for it now.' The judge returns the certificate to the court clerk without so much as casting a glance at it. 'Please continue with your argument.'

It was not something I was not ready for. I had only pulled this stunt to get my point across. This report had been acquired from a private doctor after bribing him with some extra money. I take a very attacking position to sum up the rest of my argument, dwelling at length on the statement of the child, where she had used the words 'forced on me'. This was an expression that was completely unnatural for a nine-year-old girl. It seems as if this word has been put in her mind by tutoring it to her or repeating it in front of her; otherwise, she should have been able to explain what she meant by these words. 'Actually...' I conclude my four-hour long argument, 'the accused slapped the girl several times, and while she was running away, in a bid to jump across the gate made of the thorny branches of a jujube tree, her private parts got injured, which people took for a rape. It's possible that people had not done this knowingly, because what else can be supposed to have taken place to cause such a wound in the private parts of a person? If this wound had been a result of someone sexually forcing oneself upon her, there would have been wounds or stains of semen on her uterus, or they would have found signs of semen on the labia majora and clitoris, which are allegedly said to have been lacerated. Unfortunately, on this point, the forensic report is completely silent. There is also no injury on the body of the accused, who was examined by the government doctor himself. In fact, I am surprised as to why the public prosecutor didn't try to present the girl's underwear and frock as exhibits, which would definitely have had traces of semen, which a forensic test would have confirmed or otherwise. In reality, the government doctor knew about his impotence, which is why he has maintained a studied silence on this point. The entire world knows how doctors buckle under pressure to make a strong case against the accused, favouring the public prosecutor, otherwise, there is every probability that they might lose their license. The doctor should have presented an eloquent report that could have been an example of impartiality and could have brought out the truth. Instead of taking this course, he has tried to mislead the court by presenting his incomplete and unbalanced report, which cannot be accepted under any circumstance. The girl has herself admitted that after being forced upon, she had jumped across the gate to go back home, which for a young girl, whose modesty has just been outraged by a strong man and whose vagina is bleeding, as the public prosecutor claims, is absolutely impossible. Forced sex is a very barbaric act, which can take on such an aggressive form that even young virgins break down both mentally and physically after undergoing such an ordeal and can't even move their limbs for a long time thereafter, and here we are talking about an eight-year-old child. We can't just look at the case keeping in mind simply the age of the child; we must take into account the eyewitness, as also other circumstances. As for eyewitnesses, not a single one is available, other than the child. On the other hand, even circumstantial evidence can't corroborate the charge of rape. Rather, all the facts and circumstances of the case go to establish beyond any doubt that no such incident has ever taken place. My client has been implicated in this rape case for nothing. Your Honour, I request the court to acquit my client of all the charges with respect and dignity.'

The hon'ble sessions judge looks tired after I conclude my argument. If you see it through his eyes, the courtroom must have become a darker place now. He announces the date for delivery of the judgement but settles down in his chair. He picks up some papers to study them. I know that this is just a ploy. He wants to be all by himself for a while, with a mind free from everything. The stenographer leaves his paper on the machine and goes out to have a smoke. Perhaps for the time being, he has no work to do. The court clerk has become busy with his work. The courtroom is quiet and forlorn but the judge continues to be seated between his two lamps. I gather up my papers and cast a glance at him one last time. He is sifting through some papers. Outside, the gold of sunset is dying among the trees.

'The argument wasn't bad,' Kaku comes up and whispers in my ear, 'but I can't figure out what the judge has in mind. I have come across a lot of judges, but I have never seen one like this. I can't work out his expression. And why is he so fond of darkness?'

'We have done our best. Let him do his job,' I reply. 'I need a cup of tea. I am completely exhausted.'

When a court case reaches its conclusion and the defence lawyer has no idea what is going to be the outcome of it, as a professional, it is better that he stops thinking about the case altogether and returns to some other important matter. But I don't know why this rape case has shaken me to my core. It's not because as a defence lawyer I had put in more hard work than usual, or because I adopted some unethical means, such as buying off the doctor or fabricating a false story about the accused being an impotent person or presenting a fake medical certificate as proof of his impotence, but because now, when my duty is done, I have started to see the whole case from a different perspective. Right from the beginning, it was crystal clear to me that the accused had singled out the child for the purpose of satisfying his lust. Maybe he had failed to achieve his goal. And though I had not left any stone unturned to defend him, in fact, I had adopted all the means, fair or foul, available to me. I don't know why a desire was rearing its head inside me that the rapist should get a prison sentence of some kind, be it just a symbolic one for a short duration. When I mentioned this to Kaku, he looked at me in shock.

'What are you saying?' He said, 'You have fought the case like a champion. Winning this case will get you to new heights. It was a hopeless case, but look how far have you come with it. Criminal cases have a lot of complexities. Even a murderer doesn't know if he has really committed the murder or was just a puppet in the hands of circumstances beyond his control, circumstances which are born around him but are too subtle to bring them to the eye of a judge. You have worked really very hard on this case.'

'This case was totally different,' I say. 'I won't feel bad if the accused is convicted.'

'What if he is hanged?'

'There's no chance of that. The public prosecutor should have understood that the forceful inclusion of homicide in the charge sheet was outrageous. I think the hon'ble judge had an inkling of it. I wonder why he allowed it to be included. I didn't interfere. Often, there is a chance that the case may go off the handle by the inclusion of such ridiculous charges. In such cases, often, arrows badly miss the target,' I say.

I look out of my chamber's window, where the sky is getting dark. The sun can set any moment, but I know that the lights in the Chinese Mansion would be switched on long before that. I return to my upper-floor bedroom. Mir enters with tea and biscuits, but I don't show any interest. The tea gradually turns cold. After a while, I pick up a biscuit and put it between my teeth. I don't know why, but the biscuit feels like it has no taste or flavour of its own. I fall into a deep slumber. Some clients are waiting downstairs in the visitors' room. Waking up after one hour, I take a bath and change my clothes. I go downstairs and get busy with my clients. By 8 p.m., Kaku sets off for his home. He has a habit of visiting a country liquor den before he goes home. This is an old routine. It is natural for a person whose life is hemmed in by a deep silence to take to a liquor den. I remain busy with the documents long after Kaku is gone until it is midnight. A lot of paperwork is pending. Mir comes to my room after the last client has left.

'Should I serve dinner here?' he asks. He knows what I

expect from him when I am so preoccupied with my work. I nod and place my head on the backrest of the chair and throw my pencil on the pile of documents. I take a deep breath.

'Did you spray mosquito repellent in my room?' I look at him. He has stopped at the doorway.

'I have hung the mosquito net.'

'Spray the repellent.'

I am thinking about Mir even though he is gone. Mir has been working in my house for the past seven years. He is not a regular servant. He had been an accused in a double-murder case that came my way. It had been two years since my grandfather died, and I was trying to fill the void with whatever briefs he had left behind or immersing myself in whatever civil or criminal cases that came my way. It was then that some friends of Mir came to me. These were the educated youth of our town who were in the prime of their youth. They were obsessed with Marxist ideology, but of late, they had been burning with Mao's extremist revolutionary ideas, which itself, in the long run, had paved the way for the Naxalite Movement. But the movement had lost all its steam, and to break their zeal, the state government had flooded the markets with drugs and porn. It was a preconceived and well-planned strategy of the government. Dozens of publishers had mushroomed in Kolkata on and around College Street and in its lanes and by-lanes. They were publishing and releasing books in large numbers, with stories of lust and incest, along with printed sex albums in colourful jackets. Although the political scenario was changing slowly and the very people who were once fired with high-voltage ideas of revolution had come to the helms of administration, and like old wine in a new bottle, they had also become addicted to their own power, and although, in their speeches and slogans, they still gestured allegiance to the downtrodden and poor, they had learnt all the tricks that are necessary to stick to power. So, these young people from colleges and universities had bid farewell to their education and had picked up weapons to make their revolutionary dreams come true. But it did not take long before their dream castles came crumbling down. Now, they had not only moved away from the singeing questions of society, but they had no other objective but to build up their careers by landing government jobs or earning money with whatever means at their disposal. In fact, many of those boys had landed jobs as high-ranking officers in government buildings. On the other hand, most of the Naxals had either been disposed of in fake encounters, or were locked up in jails, or were leading anonymous lives. Other young people who weren't charged with serious crimes had been let loose into society to float like rudderless boats. Mir was exactly such a boat, with no oars at its locks, one among the millions who were being pulverized in the mill of joblessness. He was the elder son of a local postmaster. Suspected of having some sort of complicity with Naxalite leaders, he had already been jailed, but with the Left Front government coming to power, all charges had been withdrawn. Now in the corridors of power, everyone expects him to work as a cog in the wheel of the supposedly revolutionary government. To all appearances, he was not leading a very bad life. His friends loved him. They hung out at a petrol pump, where they would empty bottles of cough syrup to beat the paucity of funds. It so happened one day that his father got tired of him and married him off to the daughter of his friend. Someone had suggested that once the yoke of a family is laid on his neck, not only will he be freed from the clutches of bad company, but he also will stand on his own feet. But years passed by; he fathered a child but failed to land a job. There was a real shortage of jobs those days. To make things worse, he didn't have the ability or inclination to sit for a competitive exam, a prerequisite to get a job, or perhaps it would be more accurate to say that he wasn't in the mood for it. He was a reticent and well-mannered person who would tolerate the daily taunts of his father without batting an eyelid. He had even elevated his act of hunger to the level of art. Even though he was very popular among his friends, their number was dwindling day by day. After all, they had to go forward in their journey of life. Then, one fateful night, he took out the meat cleaver from the kitchen and killed his wife and child. He also tried to commit suicide but was unsuccessful. He suffered a deep gash on his chest but narrowly escaped death. As a defence lawyer, I had seen him very closely. My father had passed away two years ago after a long coma, and my grandfather had died two months after that. I had hardly recovered from the shock of these two deaths when the case came to me. In view of the dynamics of the case, which were so unusual – after all, it was not one of your humdrum cases! – I didn't press for his bail. His friends were also of the opinion that it wouldn't be wise to get him out of prison, given his mental condition at that point in time. Later on, whenever I met him in prison, I felt as if he had no interest in the case. If one had peered into his eyes those days, one would have found oneself in a dark universe. But there would be moments when I would see a strange light flicker in his eyeballs, a phenomenon beyond my comprehension. When the prosecution case started, I got the opportunity to see his father a few times. He was a middle-aged man, calm and quiet, dedicated to his religious duties. He had not only bribed the public prosecutor to fight the case with proper diligence but had also taken the help of a famous city-based lawyer to help the prosecutor. He was scared that if Mir was acquitted, he would come after him and kill him. The odds were so heavy against him that I couldn't do anything in the sessions court. He was sentenced to eight years of rigorous imprisonment. His few remaining friends arranged some money, and with the help of a senior lawyer at the high court, who was an old associate of ours, I filed an appeal.

The high court lawyer only managed to get his sentence reduced by one year. He was a very experienced lawyer. He reprimanded me for not highlighting the circumstances under which Mir had committed the murders. Had I taken resort of his mental state, this could have gone a long way in reducing the sentence in the lower court. According to him, I just bogged down myself with the witnesses without insisting on a psychiatric examination under the supervision of the court. At least I should have dwelt on the public prosecutor's complete disregard of that point. A case history of the accused could have been built up from his facial expressions, from his way of spending his life, from the things scattered around the room at the crime scene, from conversations with him and by interrogating all those people who had kept him company before the crime. Had these nuances been taken into consideration, a profile of the accused could have been prepared under the legal watch of the court, which would have been very useful for my client. I had failed to use the most effective tool available in such cases to a defence lawyer because it was obvious from the way this crime was committed that the double murder was the result of a temporary madness. Maybe, as an inexperienced lawyer, I had failed to see the case in all its minute details, not bothering to place it in the entirety of a human perspective. Every court case has its own tricks. More often than not, the action plan that you envisage while you are sitting in the comfort of your chamber completely changes its contours once you come in contact with the reality of a courtroom, where you are compelled to devise a new plan and implement the same depending upon what avenues eyewitnesses and circumstantial evidence open up for you – that is the thing that makes such nuances vital in the courtroom. In fact, sometimes, the adoption of a tactic warrants so fast an action that in the course of doing that you don't even realize whether you have committed a mistake or have unknowingly hit the nail right on its head. In the latter case, though there is nothing in it to your credit, people pay you compliments for being such a damn success.

So, Mir was sent to jail, and people stopped thinking about him. But it was no ordinary case for me. That case made my name echo in the legal corridors of the district, ensuring that my practice as a criminal lawyer got a big boost. After this case, I got clientele in large numbers. It was a time when I was so immersed in my work that I had no time for anything else. Several years passed as such. I had forgotten Mir completely when, one day, he suddenly turned up at my doorstep. Almost half of his long and thick hair had turned grey. His facial features showed a clear imprint of hard labour in jail. Kaku took some time to recognize him. But no sooner had he recognized him than he called the police station, and a police jeep came running to our gate. I saved Mir from the police. There was still that terror and light lurking in his eyes that, during the court proceedings, I had always found in flashes, which was something beyond my comprehension. I could understand the terror, but it was more important that I should reach the depth of that light. Maybe he was indebted to me because, when fighting his case, I had not bothered about money. Rather, it can be said that I had defended him without charging a penny. But perhaps there was another reason. And I have no qualms about admitting that this so-called magnanimity of mine does not run in my blood. Both my father and grandfather were die-hard professionals when it came to practice, who would not hesitate to grab the lands and properties of their clients as a way of compensation when it came to fighting their cases. Despite strong protests from Kaku, I allowed Mir to stay in my house. He was not tight-lipped, but he was not the communicative type either. All day long, he would remain busy in the garden, but come night, and he would weep copiously in the privacy of his room, reminiscing about his childhood. Those were the days when, one morning, he spotted Jhabra and brought him home. He tended to his wounds and put a collar around his neck. He gradually took over all the household chores, and soon, the house became his entire world. As of today, I am so used to Mir that I don't think I can do without him. Kaku's doubts about him still persist, which makes him, every now and then, cast a furtive glance at Mir. Perhaps he has a gut feeling that one day he will arrive in the morning to find my throat slit open. But his opinion about Mir has slowly changed. Mir has been to Kaku's house several times. I came to know that he is teaching his son how to play guitar.

Mir is still on my mind when I come out to the veranda. It is a long veranda, looking down at the garden. At present, a light bulb out of three lamp brackets that jut out of the wall is lit, and in its eerie light, a lizard is stuck to the ceiling as if it were made of plastic. What must the rapist be doing right now inside his prison cell? The girl must have fallen asleep hugging her mother. Aisha... what is she doing now? I've had no occasion to see her in a night dress, but I know that a mother of three must look older in such clothes. Her well-formed breasts must be sagging. I don't know why, but from my childhood days, I've fancied only older women. They are the ones who always ignite my sexual yearnings.

The next day, I don't go to the court. I didn't sleep a wink last night. I send Kaku to the court to get adjournments for all the pending cases. The hon'ble session judge has taken a week to deliver his judgement. In the afternoon, I doze off in my chair. When I wake up, I don't feel like remaining indoors. I have a light lunch and set off for the river. The sun has gone down the horizon, but daylight is going to stay a while in the sky. This is the season of *palash* flowers, which are coated with winter dust. In the swamp, the reeds are blooming with bowl-shaped flowers that belong to creepers and plants that climb the reeds. Far off in the north, along the riverbank, a series of high and low hillocks are visible. People flock there for picnics. I have visited those places. It is picnic season right now. There are clumps of trees standing on the slope as also in the fields running uphill to the hillocks by the riverbank. There are eucalyptus trees too, on the plains between the hillocks and the river, planted by the Forest Department. They grow fast, and once they reach their full height, they are chopped down. Picnickers pitch their tents on these plains. There are also a few *sal*, *palash* and other wild growth standing here and there. They are disappearing gradually, falling prey to the greed of local people. To take cover from the sun, people take shelter in the shadow of whatever trees are left. They carve their names on the barks, as also the names of their beloved, but with the passing of time, the letters lose their shapes, getting crooked beyond recognition. To be honest, most of the nearby plains are infertile. They are all rocks and stones.

I stop at a place and savour the silence of the area. This is a weird silence, occasionally broken by the chirping of birds. Perhaps the silence has its own story to tell that the birds are eager to listen to. I recall my childhood friends, whom I rarely see now. I am trying to recall their names when I hear screams and laughter. At the confluence of the river, there are rows of huts by a garbage dump. Some people are gambling at a concrete platform there. It's in their nature to pester every passer-by. I know them from my childhood days. They sit there and gamble and holler until sunset, and though at a point in time they become one with the darkness, they still stick to their deck of cards. I aim to take a turn when I become aware of a silhouette behind me. I turn over and look.

Standing stock-still, a tall man is staring at me. To be honest, if it were not for his eyes glinting, I would not have been able to make out his face. I suddenly recognize him.

'I remember you. We have met earlier,' I say. 'You had lost your pet cat.'

'Payal is dead.' I hear the sub-inspector's booming voice. 'But I am grateful that you remember her.'

'It's nice to see you again.' I extend my hand, which he holds for a second and leaves. His eyes wander over the riverbank, where lights are coming up. 'You say that Payal is dead? It is weirdly dark over here. Let us sit somewhere where there is enough light. I am so curious about Payal.'

'Payal is dead,' he repeats. 'My house is nearby. We can go there. This place isn't safe after dark.'

'That's even better. I would love to visit your place.'

We take a narrow path with rows of dilapidated huts on both sides. Soon, it is the turn of concrete houses. We do not take long to reach a two-storeyed building. Here, the path narrows down into a tiny lane, a dim street lamp scattering shadows everywhere. The sub-inspector pulls out a bunch of keys from his shirt pocket and opens a wooden door. Someone must have pulled down the nameplate recently as there is a rectangular mark on the pillar. He switches on a light bulb as he enters the room through the door. This is a large room, half of which is occupied by a divan, but one can easily understand from the pillows and the bed sheets lying there that it is mostly used for sleeping. There are two wooden chairs in front of the divan. There is a big iron closet set against the wall on top of which lie books arranged systematically with a layer of dust on them. On the table in one corner of the room next to the window stands a water jug amidst an assortment of medicine bottles, its lid open skywards, as if it were a sort of question mark. Next to it is a plastic bottle and a few tumblers. A framed photo of Payal stands on the table with a flower vase. 'I have bought this house. Earlier, I had to come to my room from the back alley, but now, as you can see for yourself, I enter it from the front gate,' the sub-inspector starts blabbing. 'Thank god that I finally found the right people to negotiate with. Although, to be honest, it has not made any difference to my status. I must admit, though, this has brought some luxury of airiness and freedom to me. Earlier, I was living as a tenant in a single room, but now, I have two rooms, a whole veranda and the entire kitchen at my disposal. And that's not it; I no longer take a detour crossing all other people's rooms to get to mine. As you must have seen, I can enter my place directly from the road. For your information, all the other rooms are occupied by tenants. But I can't help it. They aren't going anywhere, not in my lifetime at least.'

'Yes, if I am not wrong, they are very old tenants that you cannot evict easily.' I smile and confirm it as a lawyer.

'Yes, you are right.' For the first time, I see a flicker of a smile on his lips. 'And I don't regret this. I am completely alone in this world, but once I, too, was a tenant like them. Unfortunately, the tenants don't get this. Ever since I bought this house, they have been in a panic. They think as a retired policeman I am going to use my clout to harass them; in fact, they are confused as to why I haven't taken any step so far. You are bound to face such problems if you are a policeman. People form a peculiar image of you in their minds, which isn't always a positive one. They don't express that to your face. But let it go. Let me show you my next room.'

He opens the next room door, and entering it, fumbles on the wall for the switchboard. A light bulb comes on. This is such a spooky room, filled with a number of wire cages standing on top of one another. Each cage has a cat, who is staring at us with a terrifying look in his eyes. If I am not wrong, by rough count, there are at least twelve cats in those cages. It looks like the room is being cleaned regularly, but a faint stink persists in the air.

'It is for the first time in my life that I am seeing cats confined in cages. Generally, we see birds or rabbits or guinea pigs in there.'

'This is for their protection,' he says as he pulls out a cat from a cage and caresses its back. 'I once tried to put two cats in one cage. But they would always end up fighting. So I could not help but separate them.' The old man smiles, and after putting the cat back in its cage, he switches off the light. We return to the first room. 'Why don't you take a seat?' he says. 'I had prepared my tea before leaving. Let me heat it up and bring it to the table. Believe me, I make really good tea. The only issue is that I do not add milk to it because I like to drink tea as tea. If you don't add milk, the tea does not develop a bad taste even after a long time.'

'Tea is an old weakness of mine.' I pull a chair and sit. 'But I can drink any kind of tea. I don't have any specific preference.'

And when he makes it to the kitchen through the inner veranda to heat up the tea, he switches on the light bulb in the veranda. A pale light spreads out in the cemented courtyard, where plants stand by the wall, all quiet and forlorn. This is a weird house. There are only light bulbs everywhere. No mercury light. And one room specially reserved for cats, where they are forced to spend their lives locked up in cages. Perhaps people are not wrong. A place where we live slowly takes after us. Who knows what is the purpose of locking up cats like this? This talk of their safety is complete nonsense. Perhaps my old friend is playing some kind of trick with these cats. It's evident that he loves cats, but this doesn't mean that you have a right to rob them of their freedom.

The owner of the house turns up with two cups on a tray, steam rising from them. 'Perhaps you are thinking about the cats, so unjustly incarcerated by me,' he says as he sets down the tray on the table. 'I like a life of solitude, and in this way, the cats don't disturb it.' He picks up a cup from the tray and hands it to me. I take a sip. The tea is sapid, flavourful. He has been able to read what is going on in my mind. I am not surprised at this. After all, he had worked as a policeman. 'You can thank me for the tea; I won't mind it.' He smiles and picks up his own cup. 'Let me admit that it has been a long time since someone has come to my house. Only a few of my colleagues are still alive. They seldom step out of their homes.'

'Thank you.' I put down the cup on an empty chair and look at him. 'You are a really good tea maker. I would like to sip it slowly.'

'This is nothing but the magic of tea leaves.' He smiles. He takes a swig from his cup. 'I have a fair amount of knowledge about tea leaves. In a way, you can say that I am adept at identifying them. Every person who is used to spending his life alone, one way or another ends up learning one or two tricks in his life. But you are the first person who has said this to me. Most people don't like my tea.'

'Because they have no idea about tea,' I laugh. 'Most people are used to gulping down milk in the name of tea, and you may count me one among them.'

'You are absolutely right. Or it would be more appropriate to say that most people have a taste for milk, just like cats.' He looks up at the other room. 'I regret keeping the cats in those cages. But after Payal's incident, I have been forced to do this. I know that this isn't the right way to keep cats, and to some extent, it's even inhuman. But believe me, I really look after them very well. Their bellies are always full. I also take them to the veterinary doctor when they are unwell. In fact, Iftikhar goes so far as to catch mice and bring them here. He uses a mousetrap for this purpose. I have segregated the males from the females, but at times, I allow them to intermingle so that they can satisfy their natural urges. I think I just mentioned Iftikhar. He is a poor boy from the neighbourhood who helps me in the upkeep of these animals. You see, a substantial part of my pension goes towards the maintenance of these cats. But I don't regret this.'

For some minutes, we sip our tea in silence. At last, I set down the cup on the tray and look enquiringly at him. 'You were going to tell me about something that happened to Payal?'

'Payal is no more.' Holding his cup in his hand, he is staring intensely at the wall where the shadow of my head falls. 'But this is a long story. I don't know whether you will be interested in this or not.'

'I would like to listen.' I again pick up my cup. A few sips are left in it. 'Had she really returned to you before she met her maker?'

'No, that isn't the case.' He sets his empty cup down on the tray. 'The gist of the story is, by the time I came to know that her death was an outcome of a sort of rivalry, it was too late to act. But I think I should narrate Payal's story from the beginning; otherwise, you may misunderstand me. Do you have time for that? I have worked out some information about you. You are a famous lawyer. People say your name with respect. Your time may be precious.'

'Yes, my job takes up a lot of my time. But I also have a life outside this job, where I have no dearth of time,' I set the empty cup down on the tray, 'and honestly speaking, I am not that famous either. Most of the clients I represent in criminal cases get sentences.'

'You can't measure your success or failure by these things,' he says. 'Fame does not come to a man for nothing, and even if it does, it doesn't stay long. You have to prove your worth, and for that, you have no option but to work hard, giving a lot of time to it. But your case is different. To be honest, I often made plans to come to your chamber. In fact, once I made it almost to the drain near the Chinese Mansion. But then I thought deeply about it and concluded that perhaps the riverbank is the most ideal place for people like us. And look, I ran into you today.'

'Absolutely.' I nod. 'Everything has its own special place and time. To be completely honest, I wouldn't have liked it if you had come to my chamber. So, you were telling me something about Payal?'

'Yes, Payal,' he says. 'I want to start from the beginning when Payal went out for the first time and did not return. And since you have enough time on your hands, I will try to narrate the incident in all its details as I saw them and felt about them at the relevant moment.'

You can recall our first meeting when I had told you about Payal's homecoming. I don't think anyone could have been as happy with her return as I was then. Three days before that, in order to save time, I was jumping across the sewer of the Chinese Mansion with my pants folded up when

Payal, in a bid to emulate me, tried to do the same and was taken away by the current. Payal really was so small that in winter days, when I was of a habit to put her in my coat pocket, she would stick out her head to look around with extreme self-pride. As I have told you earlier, this overcoat is a memento of the days when I was in service as an assistant sub-inspector of police, and although all the pomp and glory of a police officer is long gone, I don't know why it was that she would take such pride in me. I had always taken proper care of her, never allowing her to mix with her street friends, but that did not prevent her one day from following my bidding. But – and you were not wrong there – you cannot trust a cat's nature, especially when you have gotten really used to their presence.

But this time, when I cast a look at her, she not only sent shivers down my spine but also shook my self-confidence terribly. Instead of jumping straight onto the divan and hunkering down in her specific corner so that she could concentrate on her unique method of catching an imaginary rat by raising both her paws in the air, which was her habit, what happened was a sheer puzzle to me. As if it were not enough, she didn't take a single step forward from where she was. All she did was place her head on the floor in between her paws and stare at me with her mysterious eyes. It so baffled me that I pushed my chair back, and reaching her, poked the tip of my walking stick into her nostril.

Ah! Poor Payal, how thoroughly she had changed. Her hair had become soft, a glint had come to it, as if someone had taken proper care of her with a brush. She lifted her head and looked at me, and after taking two steps forward, placed her right paw on my left shoe, as if all she wanted was to be done with her responsibility. This done, she returned to her previous position. I used my selfish trick, and after filling her usual bowl with milk, placed it in front of her. She cast a glance at the bowl, plunged her nose in the milk and started to slurp it. She couldn't finish the bowl. That meant her stomach was already full. Someone must have taken care of her hunger. 'Go to your place, Payal,' I said, twisting her ear. And like a shadow, she slithered down the floor without making any fuss and went to her corner. The corner had become dark, and the alarm clock on the table was ticking away, telling us how much closer we had come to our graves.

The day was at its end. It looked like Payal was in deep sleep on the floor when she jumped up and came crawling to me, twisting her tail in the lamplight. She was staring out of the window, where it was pitch-dark. 'Are you all right?' I said, dropping the book in my lap. Her pointed ears had become tense as if she was sounding something in the air. Once in a while, she would bare her gums and yawn. For a few seconds, using her dainty paws, she kept scratching the floor while sweeping it with her tail. She tried to meow piteously, but her voice died midway. She turned around and reached the door. On the way back, she stopped under the window and looked through its iron bars into the darkness. She turned around again, regarded me for the last time and… crept through the window out into the night.

So, it was obvious that she had fallen under someone's spell. And what a coincidence that right at that time, I came across you. To be honest, it was our meeting that started casting shadows on my thoughts. No wonder I believe now that every cat has a secret life, and it is impossible for a human being to delve into it. Just try to peer into her blue eyes; you will not find any trace of emotion. You may give her a nice pet name; she won't be grateful for that. You may comb her hair giving her a presentable look, but don't expect anything in return for such things. Mice…? You are completely wrong there. She doesn't catch rodents to help us; it is in her nature that she does these things. No wonder that her transformation in such a short period was not a rare occurrence.

'I know…' I held her front paws and dangled her in front of me, 'you come back every other day because you are used to this place. Your feet drag you here, don't they? Isn't it? I don't know. But I will see to it that you come to your senses as early as possible. Got it? No, then forget it. You will get it very soon.' I put my share of kheer before her. I had brought it from the Punjabi dhaba. She licked the bowl clean and went away. She came again the next day and the third day as well, and then, on the fourth day, she refused to take the pie. 'So, you don't come here driven by your hunger, nor do you come out of greed, do you?' I said, setting her down on the table in front of the lamp where her framed photograph stands. A cat baring her teeth before the cameraman in a nasty chuckle. 'But, Miss, where are you staying these days? Who are these people? We will find out.'

That day, I decided to finish the game once and for all. To be honest, it was you who had put the idea in my head. I also looked high and low for you. I could have used your help, but by then, who knows what world you had disappeared into. So, one day, I set out alone in her pursuit. But this stalking wasn't an easy task. She would disappear in the blink of an eye. That's why I had to complete my mission in instalments; in fact, it took several weeks for me to finish the expedition. Now if I arrange these instalments in chronological order, they would look like these:

She led me straight to the street and disappeared.

She turned around at an intersection and, crossing a shop, disappeared. She stopped at the gate of a neighbourhood mosque and disappeared. She passed by the clock tower and disappeared.

She turned her head to size me up and disappeared.

She tried to send me back by digging her claws into the earth and disappeared.

She jumped over the railway tracks, and squeezing

through some hole in the fence or crouching behind it, disappeared.

She pretended to go back home and disappeared.

She continued to disappear like that for days on end, but I kept following her. I could always be found at the spot where she had vanished the last time. Finally, one day, we reached the lower end of the city, where there was a web of railway tracks. There, next to a railway line, at the end of a meadow, she vanished through a door of a railway quarter, which had a tiled roof. Light was coming out of its window as if laces were hanging on the fence. Payal had disappeared through a hole in this fence, slipping under the door curtain.

'Pinky!' A child's cheerful shriek filled the air. 'Where had you been, my Pinky? My darling, sweet, tiny Pinky! My darling, sweet, tiny, fat, innocent Pinky!' I stood quiet and forlorn for a while, and then I lifted the curtain and entered the room. After all, I once used to be a policeman. I felt no hesitation in violating someone's privacy.

This gloomy room was the abode of a lower division clerk. Right in the middle of it was an oval table that stood with an oil lamp burning on it. At one end of the table was a middle-aged man with long, dishevelled hair and a pointy forehead. He was reading a newspaper. In a corner, between a writing table and a closet, an old woman stood, bending over an *angithi*. She was putting coal in it while by the door sat an extremely slender child on a wooden box.

Payal was in his lap. He was flipping through the pages of a schoolbook. He was so thin that he reminded me of a pencil. But his eyes, my god, I am not going to forget them ever, I had never seen such large eyes in my life.

Sensing my presence in the room, the man folded the newspaper and kept it on the table. 'Can I help you, sir?' The lenses of his glasses were lit up. The creasing lines of his face had become dark.

'Thank you! I am here just to inform you that I am the rightful owner of this cat.' I took out a snuffbox from my pocket and put a pinch in my nose. After I gained control of my breath, I once again looked at the boy. 'But can I ask you, where did you get Payal? I mean, this cat.'

'Payal? Oh, so that's Pinky's earlier name.' He stood up. 'Oof, what a lovely cat is she to bring such an esteemed person like you to our house. Please, sit down, please!' He was touching the belt of my overcoat with utmost deference, dusting some imagined specks off it. 'Ah, I can recognize liveries like this. In the old days, the police used to wear them. Today, there is barely a difference between a policeman and a commoner. Will you have some tea, sir? Perhaps you will have tea without sugar.'

'Thanks!' I said icily. 'I have only come to take possession of Payal. I only like drinking tea in my home. And you are right. I was once in the police department. But now I am a retired person and don't like mixing with people. I want my cat back, that's all. Please return her to me.'

'With pleasure, sir!'

'Abba, I rescued Pinky from a sewer. She is my cat,' the boy said, picking up Payal and holding her close to his chest. He was staring at me with hate-filled eyes.

'Just wait, Adil, what kind of talk is that?' The owner of the house turned to the boy. 'Try to understand that you are simply her custodian. Now we all know this. You shouldn't forget that we no longer live in the jungle, and as good citizens, we should respect the rule of the land.' He looked at me with imploring eyes. 'Adil is my only child. His mother passed away while she was giving birth to him. Those were terrible times for us. Just a few days back, he was in the hospital. We rush him to the hospital every other day. Doctors say his lungs are in very bad shape, but he will be fine very soon because some great new medicines are available these days. We keep him safe from the cold – doctor's order, you see! We make him wear woollen clothes even during summer.'

I expressed my sympathy and, holding Payal in the crook of my arm, triumphantly came out of the room. Striding across the meadow, I proceeded towards the city. On my way out, I had deliberately turned around to smile at those two large eyes, which were lustily staring through the curtain's parting. On my way back home, I bought some toffees and tried to stuff them into Payal's mouth. She opened her eyes sleepily, looked at me, let out a weak meow and started to suck them greedily.

'I have such a soft corner for you, Payal,' I told her as we reached home. I put her in a dark corner where she liked to nap. 'You should know, I see myself in you. Perhaps you have no idea, this is the first time in fifty years that I have found someone who is so close to my heart. Don't fall asleep, I want to pamper you.'

At night, when I was going to sleep, I pulled her inside my blanket. For a while, she kept exhaling warm breath on my shins, and after that, putting her snout on the bed, she fell asleep.

She had disappeared by the time I woke up in the morning. When she came back the next day, I found that someone had singed her nose with the stub of a cigarette.

'Go back, Payal...' I said as I put ointment on her nostrils. 'I will get you back again.' She went away. But her legs were wobbly. She was pregnant.

'You haven't taken care of her, sir,' I told the man with dishevelled hair as I entered his house. 'It looks like you people are hell-bent on ruining her. She is expecting a baby.'

'Oh no, my god!' He stood up from his chair. His face was flushed, and his eyes overflowed with joy. 'Then please promise us that you will gift one of her kittens to Adil. Adil, come here! Tell us, where have you hidden Pinky?'

'Pinky is dead, Abba,' the boy said as he drew closer. His voice had the calmness of a lake. 'A freight train passed over her this morning.'

'Oh my god!' I backed off in shock. I felt as if something

had broken inside me. 'This is very strange, in fact... in fact... it's terrifying.' A storm raged in my soul. I couldn't find words to express my feelings. 'Really? But is it possible?'

'Even if you don't believe me, Pinky is not going to return from the other world.' The boy laughed bitterly and plopped himself on the wooden box. There was no iota of doubt that it was he who must have thrown her in front of a racing train.

The evening was cold outside. I was in the meadow on my way back to the city when I turned around and found the boy at the doorstep. Pushing the curtain aside, he stood framed by the door. His thick, long hair was trembling in the wind. He let go of the curtain when he saw me turn around and, opening the gate of the fence, came out of it. Fists buried in his shorts' pockets, shoes hidden in the grass, socks clinging to the calves, a victorious smile danced in his large eyes.

'You haven't killed Payal, have you? Look... was it you? Or was it just an accident? It was definitely just an accident. What else it could be?' I asked with a heavy heart.

'Do you think I am incapable of doing even such a small thing for Pinky? Yes, I admit, I was careless. I could have stopped her from going under the train. But then I thought, what's the point in stopping her? Maybe she had no intention to go back to you, maybe it was her own idea to slip under the racing wheels. Wasn't it right, then, to let her follow her instincts? How come you see my complicity in this incident when I am not there? Aren't you happy now? What more do you want from me?'

'Ah!' I bent my head on my chest as if I were speaking to myself and then strode across the meadow towards the city. 'It does not matter now, not at all. I am just thinking about something. I am so worried.'

'So, this is Payal's story. I wouldn't have guessed that this was going to be the end of Payal, especially when she was pregnant for the first time. To be honest, I can't really understand the kid's rivalry. Are we really living in such a frightening time when children can make such drastic, terrifying decisions? Believe me, from that day, I see children in a totally different light. Perhaps you wouldn't agree with me.'

'I don't know what I should say,' I say, looking out of the window, where it is pitch-dark. 'My own childhood wasn't a normal one. Anyway, I don't really get children, especially children nowadays are so strange. Cast a look at them, and you will feel like they have come from a different planet. Be that as it may, I really regret Payal's death, and if this death is an outcome of some sort of rivalry, it's even more regrettable.'

Before I can finish my sentence, someone knocks at the door. 'It's Iftikhar. He has come with my roti.' The sub-inspector gets up from his chair and opens the door. An eleven-year-old boy enters the room. Dressed in shorts and a shirt, he has a very scared look. The straps of his slippers are loose, creating a clackety-clack sound when he walks. 'Don't be scared, Iftikhar, this is our friend. Say salaam to him.'

'As-salaam alaykum,' the boy says, lifting the back of his palm to his forehead.

'Wa-alaykum as-salaam,' I reply and fall silent.

He picks up the tray with empty cups on it and goes into the kitchen. One can hear tap water running into the basin. When he comes out, he is carrying a tiffin carrier dripping water onto the floor. The sub-inspector hands him a twenty-rupee note. 'I myself prepare the curry but get the roti from a hotel. I know Iftikhar's mother. She was only eight years old when she used to come with her mother. Iftikhar's grandmother used to look after my house in those days. She was a good woman, a little hard of hearing, but she had very sharp reflexes. Now that girl has several children of her own, Iftikhar being one of them. She comes and cooks for me when I don't keep well. You can see for yourself, I have become such an old man. It is so difficult nowadays to get servants.'

'There must be family living nearby, near or distant relatives or your office colleagues?'

'All my relatives are settled in far-off cities. For the last decade, we are no longer on talking terms,' he says, 'and I don't regret that. One or two colleagues keep visiting me. But old chaps as they are, they have their own problems – all sorts of illnesses keep plaguing them. As life prolongs, in the same proportion human suffering increases. Now the situation has come to such a stage that every morning when I wake up, I am scared to think whether any of my colleagues are still there or gone for good. But don't worry. I will make it to my grave one way or another.'

'This world is gradually turning into a lonely place.' I stand up. 'Please call me if you need any kind of help.'

'This is what I pray before God Almighty every night – let that day never come into my life when I will be in need of someone.'

As I approach my house, a light goes on in the Chinese Mansion. My own house is sunk in darkness. On the road in front of me, a weak bulb is glowing in a lamp post, its jaundiced light yielding more darkness than light. Mulling over the strange life of the retired policeman, I walk past like a shadow.

On the third day, the hon'ble sessions judge takes up his chair and for a full ten minutes, remains busy signing every page of the judgement. He also goes through his twenty-page judgement time and again. At last, he declares the rapist innocent and acquits him of all the charges. He has conceded to the point that the girl suffered a wound from the thorny branches of the gate while she was fleeing the garden. And although for these three days, I had been praying for the accused to get some kind of sentence, be it a symbolic one, I don't know why I feel so elated after winning the case. Feeling ebullient about the victory, I call Aisha. Her maid picks up the phone. She has gone off somewhere with her children. For three days, she doesn't get back to me. But I don't miss her. The day she finally returns my call, I feel as if, suddenly, a new day has dawned in my life. I inform her of my big victory.

'Really?'

'Would you like to know the details?'

'Absolutely,' she answers. 'Why don't you come here?'

'No, no. I know your son would not like me to come to your place,' I lie. The truth is that I don't care about her son. But I am a lawyer, and I know how to win an argument and how to turn the tables in my favour. 'I want to see your orchard, which you always hide from me, God knows why. We can freely talk there.'

'This isn't mango season. Right now, the entire orchard is a sort of wasteland, very lonely. There may be just a few guava and *barhal* trees there but they don't bear fruit in this season.'

'I like lonely places,' I say. 'I will send my car tomorrow. We will start for the orchard in the morning. It's not very far.'

'But my children?'

'You can bring them with you or send them to your father's house with your maid. Can't you find a little time for me?'

She remains silent. 'Nazeer will be at your gate in the morning. You can leave in the car at your convenience.' I put the receiver down.

The rapist and his father are waiting outside. I ask Kaku to deal with them. He is trying to make them cough up some extra money. This is a necessary part of his profession.

Chapter Two

THE MANGO ORCHARD IS FIFTEEN KILOMETRES FROM the city. Aisha's face is devoid of any emotion. This is an old Ambassador car from my father's time. It makes more noise than is customary on these uneven roads. The two rear tires of the car have been replaced recently. The villagers have torn down most of the roadside trees for firewood. Even if one or two stand by the roadside, their barks are completely peeled off, the trunks sharpened to a point where they look like two pencils standing on their tips. One light push on the top, and they will crumble down to the ground. This is a kind of terrorism over which the police have no control. In this part of the district, the villages have hardly one or two houses, each containing a straw dump outside. It was strange to find one or two facility wells on the way, where women are washing their laundry or a cow or two are chewing cud sitting nearby. Although the winter hasn't fully arrived, most of the ponds have dried up. The farmlands are bare, but there are nurseries here and there with golden patches of marigold.

'Wouldn't it have been better had we postponed this journey?' Aisha is avoiding my eyes.

'No. And what do you think? Is it your mango orchard that I am interested in?'

Aisha turns her head to look at me. I take her right hand. She tries to free it, but there's no sincerity in her efforts.

'I have been informed that our relatives still hover around the orchards,' she says.

'Who are you trying to convince?' I break into laughter and let her hand go. 'Me or yourself? Remember, in this world, no one has time to peep into your soul.'

'What is there inside my soul?'

'Ask yourself.'

She again turns her head and looks at me. I smile mischievously.

'Listen, Aisha, we haven't been given this life so we should lead it in accordance with the sweet will of other people. To live the way we can is our personal choice. As far as your kids are concerned, they have nothing to do with these things; they will grow up one day, grow wings and fly off into a world of their own. They are not going to look back once they are on their way. God knows what guilt is gnawing at your heart.'

'What have I done? Why should I feel guilty?'

'You can ask yourself.'

For a while, the road evens out, although the earth on both sides has become steep. There is a different kind of greenery on this side of the district. Pipes are being laid along the road. The overseer and engineers are in yellow helmets, supervising work. One of them takes off his helmet to wipe sweat off his forehead and looks at us. I feel like I know him. He ignores me. We remain silent for the rest of the journey.

The two-bedroom house in the mango orchard has been spruced up. New sheets have been laid out on the beds. There are cane chairs on the outer veranda, with a low tea table standing in the middle with a vase of colourful leaves sticking out of its spout. This is the season of dust. The trees are colourless and grimy. The caretaker of the orchard appears with tea.

'This is Munsif. He in charge of the orchard,' Aisha tells me as she makes tea. 'And this is our lawyer. He has come to take a look at the orchard. This is in connection with a court case. We won't stay very long.'

The caretaker nods and goes away. After he is gone, I look into Aisha's eyes. 'What was that façade for? There's no need to act so prim and proper.'

'You may tell me about your court case.'

'It was a rape case involving an eight-year-old girl.' She lifts her head to stare at me. 'In the end, my client was found innocent.'

'So, the accusation was false.' Aisha busies herself in making tea.

'No,' I reply, 'the girl had really been raped.'

'People are not wrong when they say that you lawyers will go to hell.' She looks at me as she pushes a teacup on the table. 'You shouldn't have helped such a man.'

'You mean I should have taken the judge's place,' I say.

'Every court case is a battle between truth and falsehood. We defence lawyers are the acid that brings the truth to the surface. Had it not been so, justice would have become a one-sided affair. Without us, the law would just mow down the citizens like a blind machine.'

'I don't understand what you are trying to say,' she says, sipping her tea. 'Maybe you are right. Maybe you have your own strong reasons. But how can you defend a client once it becomes clear to you that he is guilty?'

'I only realized it at the end of the case.'

'Had this incident of rape taken place in front of your eyes, would you still have taken up this case as a defence lawyer?'

'No,' I answer. 'Then I would be an eyewitness. It is absolutely necessary for a defence lawyer, a government-appointed lawyer or a judge to be a complete outsider. No one has the right to get emotionally involved in a case. That might lead to the downright miscarriage of justice. The foundation of a just society is laid entirely on a justice system that is completely impartial.'

'Maybe you are talking about the blindfolded statue holding scales in her hand, right?' She smiles. 'Every time I see that statue, I can't help smiling. It looks like I am looking at a blind man who has no vision. How does he know which side the scales are tipping? Does it really create the impression that everyone is equal in the eyes of the law? Does such a justice system exist in our country?'

'Absolutely. People can be bad but not the system. Any

system can be wrongfully used by an individual or society or a government, as it is happening now in our country, but this has been going on since the Day of Creation and will continue until the Day of Judgment, and I admit that by no stretch of imagination am I pure. My profession is replete with flaws and weaknesses and compromised by many unfair demands. But we can't deny the fact that the strength of the foundation of democracy in any country depends on its judicial system and its independence. It's obvious that if the judiciary is doing its job well, the fascists cannot sleep a wink. They will face a lot of trouble in forcing their horrible agenda on the people. So, what else can they do if not take the reins of justice into their own hands and enact such laws as to turn the instrument of justice into a tool of torture? On the other hand, a partial and dishonest judge is worse than a murderer, a terrorist or a rapist. It's possible that his dishonesty is out of greed for money or for a high government position post-retirement because every government dangles bones before such judges. The truth is that a murderer kills one person, but a dishonest judge kills the whole system. What we need is to identify such judges and bring them to their befitting end.'

'Sometimes I am so afraid of you.' She stares at me with horror. 'And to think that you will not hesitate to defend such a judge too?'

'I absolutely will defend him.' I look into her eyes. 'Everyone has a right to self-defence. One must arrive at the truth whether this so-called judge is a dishonest person or not. We cannot rush when it comes to the truth, and I am saying this in a country where no sooner one is arrested, the media starts chanting, "Terrorists, murderers, rapists, hang him, hang him, hang him!"'

Some ducks emerge from the bushes and enter the pond. The surface of the pond is covered with moss. I see Munsif. He is carrying a huge tray full of fried chicken, vegetable salad and cold drinks, along with plates and glasses.

'Do you live here?' I say as I pick up a piece of chicken.

'No, sir. I go back home every evening. My village is right across the gate. The guard appointed by the panchayat sleeps here on the veranda. He is also from our village. He has become very old, but his eyes still work.'

'I have seen your village. There are only two or three houses there. By the way, if we stay the night, I am sure food can be arranged, right?'

'No, no, we can't stay the night,' Aisha interrupts me. 'Munsif *Chacha*, have they been coming here?'

'They come regularly, *beta*. But they don't scare me. Sometimes, they try to give me tips, but I always decline them. I have made it plain to them that I can't betray my *daughter*.'

It is obvious that the scoundrel takes money from them.

After he is gone, we continue to drink tea in silence and then move out to get some fresh air under the mango trees. The trees here are very old, overrun with mildew. Innumerable branches have snapped off from their trunks.

They are lying pell-mell on the ground. The shadows of the trees are motionless. The orchard is spread out over a large area, roughly a quarter mile, veering off to the river.

'Such a huge orchard!' I say. 'And you say that there is barely any income from it.'

'I don't lie,' Aisha replies. 'Most of the trees are too old to bear fruit. They hardly ever flower. The case is sub judice, so we can't sell their wood. They always keep an eye on our activities. I can't trust Munsif. And that elderly guard he was talking about, he is a scoundrel to his bone.'

She stops. We stand surrounded by trees. Aisha peeps into my eyes valiantly. I give her my hand, which she holds.

'Don't be scared,' I tell her. 'I am not a bad person. I won't take any step without your consent, and anyway, I am serious when I say I want to marry you.'

'And Nadir? I am scared of him. I have never seen him so quiet as he is nowadays.'

'I can understand him.' As I feel the push of her soft breasts on my chest, I pick up a lock of hair from her face and plant a swift kiss on her lower lip. She tries to turn away but can't. My second kiss is much longer. Her heart is beating. We return. The caretaker is nowhere. I drop Aisha to her room so that she can rest for a bit. I come out alone for a stroll among the trees. With the bright sunshine, it's a little hot here. I walk along the pond and reach a small village. There is a handful of bamboo groves there, with mud huts around. There are also cows tied to the trunks of betel nut trees. Behind the village, there are vegetable fields fenced in by bamboo and then rows of mango trees. Aisha had told me that in the past, hyenas used to come here from the nearby forest.

As if this world is not bad enough for human beings!

I come back. Aisha has bolted her door from the inside. Maybe she is taking a nap. I sit in the next room on a wooden chair and stare out of the window. I realize that my coming here has served no purpose. And this orchard, there is really nothing worthwhile here. I assess the failure of my excursion when I see Aisha at the door. Her hair is dishevelled, and a corner of her sari has slipped off her body. Her eyes show that she is in deep shock.

'I just saw him?' Her voice is quivering. 'Who?'

'Nadir. He is roaming around.'

I get up and move her away from the door to go outside. I head towards the Ambassador car which is parked in the shade of a tree just inside the gate.

'Nazeer, have you seen a sixteen-year-old boy? Do you recognize Madam's son?'

'Yes, sir, I recognize him. But I have not seen him, sir.' Nazeer is in the back seat, where he is resting. He wipes his sweaty face with a handkerchief.

'If you see him anywhere around, immediately inform me.'

Despite alerting him, I myself take a few rounds of the place. Aisha must have been imagining things.

When I return, Aisha is sitting on her bed.

'What will happen now?' She looks at me helplessly.

'You are getting scared for no reason,' I say. 'Let's go back. You were right. We shouldn't have come here. There is no Nadir outside. You are a scared woman fantasizing about things.'

'I saw him with my own eyes. He was on his motorcycle.'

'You might have.' I shrug carelessly. 'Sometimes, our eyes show us the things that we want to see.'

'Believe me.'

'I do.'

We return in the car. On our way, God knows when, Aisha takes my right hand and places it in her lap. I let it be there but avoid her gaze.

Three days after the incident, I get a call from Aisha. She is crying inconsolably. 'He has made my life hell,' she tells me.

'Did he hit you?'

'No.' It's clear from her tone that she is lying. 'Did he say something?'

'No.'

'Aisha, then how can he make your life hell?' I lose my patience over the phone. 'You are behaving as if you have committed some sin.'

'I have committed a sin.'

'I am coming to you. We should clear things up with Nadir.'

But when I cross the river and reach her house, there is no trace of Nadir anywhere. She hugs me and cries incessantly. 'I don't want to lose my child.'

'What do you mean?'

'What if he has left home and gone for good?'

'He won't go anywhere,' I say. 'Let him return. I will talk to him. And if he objects to our marriage, I will stop coming here. You will find another lawyer. I will hand over all the briefs to him. Are you happy now?'

She is staring at me with eyes brimming with tears. The more she tries to stop her tears, the more they flow down her cheeks. She rests her head on my chest and starts crying.

'Forgive me. I don't want to lose you. I had no inkling that he would behave like this. It's not your fault at all.'

'Nor is it the fault of that poor fellow.' I caress her cheek. 'Anyone else in his shoes would have done the same thing. By the way, my instinct says if I talk it out with him, everything will be fine.'

'No, no!' she says, pulling herself away. 'Not now. You don't know Nadir. He is a different kind of kid. No one has ever seen him cry. But I know he hides in the bathroom and cries there all by himself.'

She wipes her tears with the edge of her dupatta and brings tea for me. I look at her in silence as I sip my tea. She returns my look without batting an eyelid. The church bells toll at a distance.

It is pitch-dark by the time I reach the river. The few remaining bulbs on the wooden poles burn like butterflies with their wings spread out. The electricity goes out by the time I reach the big rock. A lantern hangs from the thatched roof, where people are moving like shadows. The riverbank is empty. After waiting for a long time, I see a rickshaw. It is coming from the direction of the city, but there are people in it. I wait for its return. Time passes; it doesn't come back. Rickshaw pullers don't want to come to this side of the river after sunset, or they come very infrequently. I am forced to descend to the dry riverbed and plough through the sand. At night, you can't take long strides in the riverbed. You have to measure every step carefully, else some piece of rock or dry wood or skeleton of some animal can injure your leg. Occasionally, I stop on my way and wait for the rickshaw to pull up. But this is so strange. Usually, rickshaw pullers don't take so long to return. They don't get passengers for the city at this time, and despite the fact that they don't come to this side of the river without taking return fare, they would not lose a passenger. But it's quite late. It's possible the rickshaw puller lives on this side of the river. I don't have any option but to cross the river on foot. It's not the first time I am doing that. I have crossed this river many times, even in darkness. It's not that difficult. It just takes a little longer. As I walk, I see stars gleaming in the sky, while across the river, the city is buried in darkness. The facility poles emit no light. It will be at least two hours before the electricity returns, or perhaps more. After walking a while, I reach the first current of water. This is the middle part of the river. After this, there are two more currents. I crouch at the water's edge and take off my shoes when I feel that someone is calling me. Still squatting on the sand, I turn my head. At first, I see nothing in the dark, but then slowly, the silhouette of a man becomes visible. A distant red light is burning on his head. Maybe he is smoking a cigarette. He stops some fifteen steps away. Meanwhile, I have taken off my shoes and socks. I stand up. Out of habit, I stuff my socks into the shoes.

'I was saying that someone has punctured the poor rickshaw puller's tires.' The man speaks up, taking a puff of his cigarette. 'How terrible for you. You have no idea what kind of people roam about this side of the river at night.'

'I know. I have always been crossing this river after sunset,' I yell. My sixth sense as a lawyer tells me that something is wrong. But I don't panic.

'Which you shouldn't.' He takes the cigarette from his lips and flicks off the ash. I can see sparks fly in the air. He takes some more steps to come closer, but he is still a silhouette to me with no ears or nose. I wonder if he also sees me as a silhouette.

'I am a lawyer,' I say. 'Do you recognize me? Are you also going to the city?'

'No one is going anywhere.' I hear a gruff voice, and some more silhouettes shimmer at the surface of the water. Perhaps there is only one option left for me. I should throw my shoes and take to my heels. But instead of running away, I plod slowly. I know I can't run with my calves buried in water.

If I do so, I might lose my balance and fall through the soft sand. In addition to the splashing sounds of water that my legs are making, I overhear other human legs splashing water behind me. I know the water isn't very deep, no higher than my ankles or calves depending upon the place, but there might be a pothole or two where I may trip and go down crashing. They will definitely catch up with me if they have bad intentions. The riverbank is too far. But there is no hurry in their pace, as if they are merely crossing the river. I finally come to a stop, turn around and look at them. All the silhouettes stop forthwith.

'You tire us out for no reason.' The silhouette smoking the cigarette flicks ash again into the water.

'What do you guys want?' At thit point, when all of us are standing still in the water, I take off my wristwatch and dangle it in front of them while with my other hand, I get my wallet out of my pocket. 'I only have this watch and this wallet with me right now. There must be around five hundred rupees or more in it. You can take it. No, wait, I also have a gold ring. I assure you I am not going to report it to the police.' I start to pull the gold ring from my finger.

Someone laughs loudly.

'Take these, take these!' I extend both my hands. The silhouettes stand still, as if pondering over something. It's obvious they aren't muggers. 'Whoever you guys are, I want to tell you that I am a criminal lawyer. This may create problems for you. Can't we go to some other place where there is enough light?'

'Light!' I hear laughter a second time. 'Who needs light?' I feel like they are tightening their circle around me. And now I stand surrounded by them. They are breathing heavily. Someone makes splashing sounds in the water as he changes his position. This further deepens the gloom. The contours of faces, though still hazy, are slowly becoming visible. It's a strange vision. A few human silhouettes stand in the water, the stars gleaming in the sky and the city across the river sunk in darkness. Who is going to bother about what is going to happen to a man in the middle of a river? 'Okay then.' I give up and raise both my hands above my head. 'We may talk standing here.'

'Yes... this is a nice place for a chat.' One of the silhouettes lifts his finger at me. But it is someone else behind me he is pointing out. I turn around to see who it is, but just then, millions of stars explode in my eyes. Holding the back of my head with both hands, I kneel in the water. As the water courses through my pants, filling them completely, I feel another thud at the back of my head. I hold my head, the warm blood coursing through my fingers. Holding my head with one hand, I try to stand up, when my back and shoulders receive continuous blows. Despite all these hits, I somehow manage to stand up when someone kicks at my back, pushing me down again. This time, I plunge into the cold water. I am trying to keep myself above water when someone grabs hold of my leg and drags me through the water to carry me to the sand. My eyes are dark, and the stars swim across them. The blood gushing out of my forehead is blinding me. I attempt to hold myself but keep sinking down. I feel the sandy water in my throat. An unbearable pain shoots through my shoulders and legs as if my arteries will implode. I have been dumped in the sand. The voices of people towering over me are clearly audible. Some sort of argument is going on between them. Poking my fingers into my eyes, I try to make out the world around, but either I have lost my eyesight or the darkness has enveloped them. I am mumbling in protest when someone bends over me, and a strong splash of liquid hits my face. A face looms out of the darkness.

'Nadir!' I hear my own scream before it dies out. I try to catch hold of it, but the silhouette steps back. The darkness completely fills my field of vision. Once again, I am at the mercy of blows. I hear my bones crack. A searing pain rips through my head. There is a buzzing sound in my ears. Someone is again dragging me back into the water, this time grasping me by my hair.

I wake up with severe pain in my bones. Above is a firmament full of gleaming stars; underneath, I lie completely naked on the sand at the edge of the water. There isn't a shred of clothing on my body. My back and hips are icy cold. I try to sit up. Such a vast universe, and I, a human being, all alone in the sand. I feel my head; there is no wound there. I try to stand up, and I am surprised to see that both my legs are fine. But what about my clothes?

The river is empty in front of me. Behind my back, everything is buried in darkness. I have no option but to move forward and, leaving the river behind, I make my way to the house. My wobbly legs don't get much support from the sand. I manage to somehow cover the distance. Then I sit down and look straight ahead. There is no human being around, no light anywhere that I could yell at for help. Water is shimmering in the distance in a straight line. I stand up and try to walk. The crunching sand sends a shiver through my soul to every pore of my body, as if my entire being is overflowing with sand, and any time now, it will start pouring out of my ears and nostrils. A large moon emerges from the cityscape and shines much lower than usual. This moon is so large that I don't think I will ever be able to crawl past it. But it's a strange moon; despite spreading light all around, both on the land and the sky, its own surface is dull and lifeless. It's probably a result of the moon's bright rays that the stars have become dim. Something moves in the background. I try to focus on it but fail to make out anything. But no sooner I stop looking at it, it feels as if millions of fish are staring at me through their tiny eyeholes. Is this actually the light of far-flung stars that is reaching us, ricocheting off some stars closer to the earth, or am I seeing them because, suddenly, my senses have become very acute? I find all this weird as I walk naked from head to toe, a nakedness that I don't identify with myself. I wish there is some safer way to reach the Chinese Mansion.

The Chinese Mansion! How can I reach there? What necessity pulls me there? All I need is the security of my home. Strange that the river is spread so far out to the horizon. This river is not something that would have come into existence in one day. Then why am I seeing it like this? Perhaps I have no other option but to keep dragging my feet, thinking about these odd things or keeping them off my mind. The Chinese Mansion... whatever the cost, I must find it. It's my last hope in a dark universe. My house will be somewhere close to it.

There is moonlight on the sand. I don't know how far I have come. I discover black patches here and there, maybe leftovers of bonfires. Maybe people come here for picnics, or perhaps the dead are cremated here. If it's the latter, then I must be somewhere by the cremation ground at the bank of the river. My feet are damp. I find myself standing naked at the steps of the cremation ground. I am besmeared with mud and sand. A little way off, a pyre is burning on the sand; the dead body appears to have been completely charred. A man is pouring water on the pyre from a tilted earthen pot. Finally, the pyre turns cold. The clay pot is broken into pieces. They also break the funereal cot and walk along the river. Sitting alone at the step of cremation ground, I see them liquefy into silhouettes. I don't know how much time has passed. The silhouettes are not visible, or maybe they have merged with the trees and plants swaying in the horizon. Time to go home. I am still naked from top to toe. It's true that the city is pitch-dark, but the moon is shining in the sky with all its brilliance. I must find a safe route away from the sight of people, lest people see me stark naked. Perhaps I have no other option but to wait till the moon is gone. After all, it is not going to stay forever in the sky. If I have to reach home, the night must be dark. And then, sitting naked on the ghat, I recall the forest behind the Chinese Mansion. I only have this one route left to reach somewhere closer to my home without someone spotting me. Hardly a second has elapsed when I find myself in the forest. I walk on dry leaves that make crunchy noises under my soles. Fireflies are crawling on the leaves of a low branch. I see a row of trees, whose lower ends are lit up by some eerie light. My god! Is it the Chinese Mansion that is leading me? Walking under the trees, am I on the right track? The trees are getting thicker. The moon has climbed up a good distance in the sky. It looks so small, as if it is melting like ice. Though it is autumn, when the forest abounds with thorns and splinters, they have no effect on my bare soles. I have never entered this part of the forest before, and today, when I have, I am completely at a loss... at a loss, alone and naked. Who knows whether this is going to end up at the Chinese Mansion or someplace else? My feet are numb. I am walking barefoot for the first time in my life. It was fine so long as I was on the sand, but now I am on a forest floor teeming with snakes and scorpions. I am slowly losing energy. The muscles of my legs have become numb. The thorns and stones have started to stab my soles. Tripping and falling over bushes and thorny branches, I am losing my breath. And as I go through this ordeal, I feel as if I am surrounded by people. Several lanterns pass by. This is a caravan of Chinese people, all naked from top to toe. Gripping lanterns in their hands, they overtake me without so much as casting a cursory glance. I tread on their heels. And soon, I feel like I am also walking in a circle. We all keep coming back to the same spot. It looks like I will never be able to come out of this circle. It is strange. In the beginning, I was at its tail end, but soon, the circle closes. Gradually, it picks up speed, and turning faster and faster, it becomes a whirlpool. The lanterns are brightening up the tree trunks. Leaves and bushes are on fire. It looks like this circle will go round and round for all times to come. My god! Have I become a part of spirits bent on circumnavigating the universe for all eternity?

I try to get out of the circle, but every time I do that, it pulls me back. Ultimately, I have no other option but to try and stand still. But that is no longer in my power. I continue to revolve until it sends my head reeling. I feel like I will collapse on the ground any time. I let out a shriek.

There is white light all around me. This is a hospital bedroom. I am bandaged from top to toe. Drenched all over in sweat, I am breathing heavily.

Other patients are staring at me from their beds. Most of the faces have oxygen masks on them. All the bodies are motionless. I hear human voices as if they are coming from some other planet. Slowly, the voices come close. I see two nurses. One of them lowers herself and adjusts my oxygen mask. Her nostrils protrude outward. Our eyes meet.

'Thank god, you have finally regained consciousness!'

I am in an ICU. I have been lying here unconscious for the past fifteen days. I had lost a lot of blood. One of my legs and both my arms are broken. It will take some time before they remove the oxygen mask. The next day, from the outskirts of the city, a police inspector visits me. He informs me that I was lying unconscious at the edge of the water right in the middle of the river. Some of my bandages are removed. The police have arrested the girl's father who had attacked me in the courtroom. A few of his relatives had also been taken into custody. This news hurts me. They are released after my statement. I tell the police about Nadir. I hadn't been able to recognize the others.

The nurse asks the inspector not to disturb me. On the third day, my health is a little better when he turns up again. This time, I narrate the whole incident.

'Are you sure you saw the boy at the crime scene? You said it was absolutely dark there?' He picks up his pencil from the paper and looks at me.

'Yes. But you can recognize someone you already know even if it is dark. I was injured but was conscious enough to recognize him. He spat on my face.'

'Any specific reason for this hatred?'

'His mother is my client. I look after her property cases. The boy is under the impression that something is going on between his mother and me, which is all his illusion.'

The inspector's eyes betrays that he firmly believes in an illegitimate relationship between us. Ah, our prejudices! How fast we fall prey to our herd mentality!

'She is a widow,' I say, annoyed at his reaction. 'Please don't go around telling it to the world. She is already facing a lot of hassles. She cannot deal with another problem this big. That's exactly what her relatives want.'

'But once the investigation starts, it will all come out,' he says. 'People will gradually find out everything.'

'That's the public prosecutor's business,' I say. 'Can't you mind your own?'

'I was only thinking out loud, sir,' he says with embarrassment.

'You don't have to think out loud. I have identified the right person. Treat him to your third degree, and you will get the names of the others. As far as the motive is concerned, that's your job to find. And there's no need to come here any more. I have told you everything. For the rest, you can get a test identification parade done. I will be there. I can't say anything else right now. There is a searing pain in my head.'

One more month in the hospital and I am discharged. It is deep winter now. The veranda and the walls of the house have become icy cold. I have got a new heater installed in my bedroom. I have also secured the personal services of a nurse. Her name is Kamna. I find my house so desolate and empty. In the beginning, Mir does not approve of the idea of a nurse. But he eventually accepts her presence. Right now, all I am capable of is walking a few steps with the help of crutches. The nurse is a quiet woman who has a habit of applying ample vermilion in the parting of her hair. Kamna has genuine sympathy for me. Perhaps she is surprised that this sprawling house has no woman under its roof. Everyone in the house, from the owner to the servants, is male. She has taken a liking to Mir since she first cast a glance on him, treating him like her own little brother.

'Were you very young when your mother passed away?' She breaks her silence one day, and for the first time, I realize that she is a very talkative woman.

'No. My parents had fallen foul with each other after I was born. They lived separate lives. I have no memory of my mother.'

'Are you the only child of your parents?'

'Yes,' I reply. 'People say that I was born after a lot of prayers and supplications.'

'This house badly needs a woman.' She smiles. She is knitting a sweater for me despite my telling her not to do so. She purchased wool after taking money from Mir. It does not bother her that the winter will be over by the time the sweater is ready or that I may get rid of her services long before that.

I have had my grandfather's heavy armchair brought to the courtyard. I sit in the sun and keep staring at my ruined garden. I have started to meet my clients there. The plasters on my hands and legs are yet to be removed, which is why I am still dependent on the nurse. The barber comes every day to shave me. He has grown completely old. One of his eyes has developed cataract. But his eyesight is beyond repair now. His optical nerves have completely dried up. His back has become crooked. Kamna gapes at him in wonder while he works on me.

'How can he still handle the scissors?' she asks me with surprise.

'You must have realized that when he grips the razor, his other hand puts all its weight on my skin.' I smile in return. 'As to his vision, he doesn't need any of it to do his job. Once he holds the razor, his fingers work automatically. He has done this all his life. By the way, one of his eyes is fine.'

'If you allow me, I can shave you. I mean, I don't want to take his job. You can give him his wages.'

'No, no. He is a man of my grandfather's times. I can't say no to him. As long as he is alive, this is his house. And I am afraid, he won't work for free. These old people have a lot of self-respect. They have their own principles.'

'Everything in this house is in the clutch of old times,' Kamna says and points out at the garden. 'Such a huge garden and no gardener to take care of it!'

'Our gardener died a long time ago.'

'You never think of a new man.'

'No,' I say. 'The fact is, I like abandoned gardens like this one where plants and trees grow on their own, live with a free will and die without taking any favour from an axe. You don't know how difficult it was for me to stop Mir from tampering with this garden. He is a good gardener. He has learnt gardening from his days in prison. But he has finally understood my point. So, he has accumulated many flowerpots on the roof to satisfy his passion for gardening.'

'I can see that. In this garden, most of the trees are dead, but they still stand in their places.'

'Every garden is in need of trees like these.'

One day, while Kamna stands on the terrace enjoying the sun, I gesture towards the parting of her hair.

'You love your husband a lot. I have seen very few women wear so much vermilion.'

'He suits my requirements,' Kamna says, and I am taken aback.

'What did you say? Say it again?'

'My husband is a thing of necessity for me. We see to each other's basic needs.'

'And your children?'

'I have a boy. He is a grown-up man now and lives his separate life.'

'You don't love your husband?'

'In life, it is not essential that you should fall in love.' Kamna holds a sweater a little way off from herself and studies its design. 'We human beings have been given such a short time in this world. We support each other, that is all. Why bother to take other headaches? We are satisfied with the way things are.'

'You are not answering my question. Is it not necessary that one should have some kind of love in one's life? How can two people spend their lives without some kind of love for each other or without hating each other, for that matter, if not for anything else, out of some kind of necessity? Human life is so long. Even animals, over time, develop some emotional bonds between themselves. We are, after all, human beings.'

'Believe me, there is no better arrangement than this. You can try it.' She smiles mischievously. 'Just minding your own business and waiting for the next day to begin, if that day ever comes by god's grace, and to go on contemplating that whatever is there between us is merely a professional relationship with no emotional package attached to it – not only does it cause no problem, it solves a lot of extant ones, too. You don't have to shed tears if someone dies, and if one is compelled to do it, at least the quantity of tears would be reasonable.'

'And what about your son?' I look at her completely confounded. 'How do you see him?'

'We are related by blood. And blood doesn't need words to convey messages. It says what it has to say without taking the help of words.'

'Do you know how I ended up like this?' I look into her eyes.

'If you care, you can tell me.' Her eyes are glued to her knitting needles, as if she is both interested and unconcerned at what I am going to divulge.

'The son of one of my clients suspects that some illegitimate relationship is going on between his mother and me. He conspired with his people to attack me.'

'The result of love. If he didn't love his mother beyond the limits of sanity, he wouldn't have taken such a stupid step. We rear our children in an emotionally charged atmosphere.'

'Are you sure, given the circumstances, your son wouldn't have done the same thing?'

'Maybe he would have done the same,' she says. 'But I am lucky. He doesn't live with us any more. He lives with his wife and children. Though we live apart, we take proper care of each other.'

'You are an unusual woman, Kamna.' I direct her attention towards the Chinese Mansion, whose grey roof is gleaming in the setting sun. 'Do you see that mansion? From my childhood days, I have had an acute urge to enter that house, but I never muster up enough courage to do that. Like a woman I am obsessed with but choose to stay far away from.'

'Perhaps this is the most ideal situation for you.' She casts an indifferent glance at the tiled roof of the Chinese Mansion. 'I feel that you have an acute hunger to own certain things, but it would be better for you that you never have access to them, otherwise, your dream will fall apart. You are a man who can't live without a dream. I will advise you not to enter that mansion; otherwise, it will slip away from your fingers. You will find that it is not there.'

I look at Kamna with astonished eyes, as also deep respect. I feel like I have known her for a long time. Yes, this woman has lived her entire life with me, casting her shadow on me, supporting me, whispering in my ears, and the wonder of wonders is that we are face to face for the first time in our lives.

'How long have you been living in this city? I don't think you were born here.'

'We came here many years ago. You are right, we are not native to this city. We live here in a rented house,' she says. 'We migrated from East Pakistan, which is now called Bangladesh. A short while ago, we bought a small piece of land on the outskirts of the city. My husband wants to cultivate honeybees there. He has started buying boxes.'

'Your husband? What is he?'

'He...' She laughs. 'He used to be a good poet before we migrated to India. Unfortunately, after crossing River Padma, his poetry died a sudden death. He has retired recently as a *haat chaudhari*, and now he thinks about honeybees all the time.'

'Then both of you must have a huge difference in age?'

'Yes, huge.' She starts knitting her sweater. A strange smile plays on her lips. 'I was only thirteen, a sentimental Bengali girl, heart and soul enamoured of poetry. He made me elope with him from East Pakistan. I was crazy over his poems. I wish I had known at that time that at the end of the day, in place of a poet I will have to rest content with a *haat chaudhari*.'

'Can I ask you a question?' I am trying to read her face. 'Speaking from a sexual point of view, are you happy with him?'

'Am I bound to answer this question?'

'No.'

'Thanks.' She stands up. Her face has brightened up. 'Oh god! I can't believe it. I have finished your sweater.'

'Really?' I accept the purple cardigan and examine it with surprise. 'You have finished it in time, Kamna. I can wear it even this winter.'

'Absolutely. What else was I working so hard for?' She gets up, comes to me and stands behind my back. She helps me wear the cardigan. She still has some bits to finish, some final stitches and sewing of buttons. 'The size is all right. My assignment is over.' She takes the cardigan off my back. 'Your plaster will be removed on Monday. One or two days more and you won't need any nurse.'

'No one can know my needs better than me!' I look helplessly at the garden and, taking a long sigh, close my eyes. After a while, Kamna takes off my shirt and vest and starts massaging me. Sitting on the armchair and feeling her soft hands doing their job, I doze off. Immediately, I find myself inside a forest. It's the same forest that starts behind the Chinese Mansion. This time, I am with my friends. It is about sunset, but it is already dark inside the forest. 'What do you think? Is it a good idea to come here at this time?' Sikandar whispers in my ear. He will always be the first person to air his doubts in such circumstances. Our half-yearly exam is over. We are on a short vacation. We have enough time to indulge in all sorts of useless activities. 'Why not?' I say. 'Are you scared of this place? I saw a lot of cars come to the Chinese Mansion today. This is the right time to solve its mystery.'

Above our heads, branches of trees are intermingling. The sky appears a wee bit too blue through them. Taking steps carefully in the darkness that prevails between the tree trunks, we realize that on account of last week's rain, the earth has become very soft and mushy. Probably all kinds of insects have come to the surface. Winter is here, casting its dark shadow on the earth. This isn't autumn, but many trees on the slope have begun to shed their leaves. This place has become so confusing, not only for human beings but also for the vegetable kingdom. Just like human beings, a lot of alien undergrowth has appeared, bestirring the soil. There are trees who have their own spring and their own autumn. At one place, there is a clearing in the bush; a snake has sloughed off its skin on a thorny twig. From the quiet all around, it looks like we are in a universe where sound hasn't been created yet. We stand silent and still, holding our breath when bells ring at a distance. A cat jumps from the blue on a pile of leaves in front of us. She stands still on her legs, her tail curled up in defiance. Eyes burning.

'It's the incarnation of a Chinese ghost.' Amjad picks up a stone and hurls it at her. The cat breaks into a swift run. She climbs a tree trunk as if she were prepared for it. Passing through various branches, she disappears from our sight, but wherever she goes, the rustling of leaves tells us of her hideout. Finally, she pops up at a branch high up in a tree trunk. Sitting there all quiet, she is staring at us. This is really odd. After wandering in the forest for a long time, we emerge on a plain within sight of the Chinese Mansion, where darkness has already descended. The sun has vanished in the horizon, carrying with it all its molten gold. The place looks way too ominous today, as if the land will split open and any minute a dragon may emerge, spewing fire all around. The rear gate of the mansion looks unreal, as if some child has clumsily drawn it with charcoal. It is ajar. There is a hint of bright light inside. Everything outside is enveloped in a milky darkness. The courtyard reeks of rotten leather.

'This is the right time,' Sikandar turns around and whispers into my ear. 'There won't be a better opportunity to solve the mystery of the Chinese Mansion once and for all. Are you ready to take the plunge?'

I look at him in astonishment, but ignoring the fact that this is the same Sikandar whose heckles would go up at the drop of a hat, I push open the gate. There is a small, dirty pond inside, where maybe the Chinese wash their leather. All around the pond, Chinese lanterns are burning on wooden poles. The two-storey building looks amazingly tall as we stand below it. 'The Chinese use lanterns to lead the spirits of their forefathers home,' Amjad whispers. The vigilant man inside him has woken up again. 'It is not safe to stay here.' I don't pay heed to his warning. Someone is playing a flute in the upper floor. A petromax has been kept on the ground. A polished coffin shines brightly in its light.

The coffin's lid is half-open.

We don't have the guts to look inside. Finally, it is I who step forward. I pick up the petromax when I hear some footsteps behind me. I turn around. A good number of Chinese people are standing behind with bright robes and large sleeves. They look at us blankly. Their hair is flaming, and robes are billowing in the wind. Suddenly, they bestir themselves, take wings, and rising in the air, come at us. The petromax slips from my hand. I wake up screaming. I am on my terrace, lying in my armchair. My face is drenched in sweat.

Kamna's hand gropes my shoulder. Her fingers reek of massage oil.

'Did you have a nightmare?' She is gazing at me. There is a worried look in her eyes.

'Maybe!' I reply. She picks up a towel and wipes my face. How can I tell her that this is the same dream that has been following me in various forms throughout my life!

Chapter Three

AFTER BEING TAKEN INTO CUSTODY, NADIR HAS divulged the names of all his accomplices. They have been arrested. They are Aisha's close relatives from her in-laws' side, the same people who had filed several cases against her, including the one about the mango orchard. Nadir was in cahoots with them. He had his own problem with me, and they had their own score to settle; as a result, enemies on both sides had become friends. I was afraid that one of these days Aisha and I would come face to face. But she never bothered to come to the hospital to enquire after my health. A month after my mishap, Kaku suffered a heart attack. He has been admitted in the same hospital from where I have returned. There is no other hospital in our city where one can go for serious cases. The operation theatres of all private nursing homes reek of past operations. I have not recovered completely, but I go every day to see Kaku in the hospital. One day, when I return, I see Aisha in my chamber. She is waiting for me. Sitting all alone in a chair, she looks sad and disappointed. There are grey lines in her hair. I was not expecting her. Once we are alone, she breaks down and collapses in my arms.

Feeling the soft pressure of her nipples on my weak ribs, I keep caressing her hair with a sense of relief, as if a bird has come back to its nest after a long strenuous journey. Perhaps I had taken her for something that I had lost forever.

'You want your son to be acquitted of all the charges?' Leaving her at her chair, I go back to my own. 'He did his best to kill me.'

Aisha looks at me with a blank expression in her eyes. She says nothing. Tears roll down her cheeks.

'Don't cry.' I take out my handkerchief and put it across the table. She picks it up and wipes her tears. 'We can't put a stop to the legal process. But let me see what I can do for Nadir. Anyway, he is a minor; he might be accorded a mild sentence. There is some probability also that he will be acquitted.'

'If he is sentenced to imprisonment, he will die. I have heard a lot of bad stories about jail, about hardcore criminals abusing children there. Even the prison staff doesn't stop lusting after them. For god's sake, save him. He was definitely present when the attack took place, but he did not take part in it.' Aisha is all tears. It would have been easy for me at that moment to take her to bed, but I am not that weak. I pour out water in a glass and place it before her. I get up from my chair, and after going to her, sit down at the edge of the table. I fold my hands on my chest. I stare hard at her.

'You tell me, what should I do?'

She remains silent, contemplating the documents

scattered on the table. 'Are you not hurt that he went so far as to take the help of your enemies?'

'They are our relatives. Nadir had turned this matter into a family prestige. We can't blame him entirely for this.'

'And these are those same relatives who want to see you homeless on the street.'

Perhaps Aisha has no words to fall back on. She sits still in her chair. There is a lost look in her eyes.

'Try to understand Nadir.' After a while, she wipes her eyes with my handkerchief and says in a low voice, 'He is an adult now.'

'Instead of sitting here, I could have been in my grave.'

After Aisha goes, I stroll around my terrace. The Chinese Mansion looks more ominous in the sunlight. Its rear garden is not visible due to clumps of trees. Maybe the only Chinese family in the city burns or buries their dead therein. Nadir... I am at a loss. What should I do about him? He is the most important piece in the game that is going on between Aisha and me, a pawn that has overshadowed the whole gambit. He is not just ruining the game, but he has brought it to such a delicate stage. And now that the game has come to such a complicated point, how can we overlook him?

I contact the public prosecutor. I have seen to it that he gets tipsy before I take up the matter.

'He is the most important piece in this prosecution case. Without him, the whole case will fall apart,' he says. 'I can't promise anything.'

'Any lawyer could have come up with this excuse. I had expected more acumen from you.' I express my irritation. 'I want that you have your cake and eat it too. I am sure you will be able to find a way out; you are a past master in this game. I will help you in every possible way. I want to save that child from harm, but I also don't want this case to go to the dump.' I ask the waiter to refill his glass. We are in the only club of the city, sitting over glasses of whisky. 'Do you know what I want? I want them to get the harshest possible sentence. I want the law to take its course. But we will have to save Nadir. They are going to file a bail appeal before the sessions judge. In view of his tender age, I don't see any problem in it.'

'Aren't you scared that after coming out of jail, he may cause some serious trouble for you?'

'He should get bail,' I insist. 'Give me your word that you will not raise any objection.'

'All right. I won't oppose his bail. But we are bound to set some conditions. Anyway, there is no chance that he will be out of the mess until the case is over.'

'Thanks.' I get up and shake his hand vehemently. 'Sometimes, you surprise me with your magnanimity.'

After Nadir is granted bail, one day, I resume going to Aisha's house in my car. I never find him in the house. Perhaps mother and son have come to some sort of understanding.

Aisha will always wait on her sofa, knitting her sweater. She smiles as our eyes meet. She is impatient to be led to bed. I am sure of that. But I know that would be some sort of quid pro quo for Nadir's sake because the criminal case has not yet started, whereas I want Aisha all to myself. I don't stay too long at Aisha's house. Every time Nazeer opens the back door of my car, I feel like Nadir is lurking somewhere very close, maybe following me all the while. Nazeer doesn't like this place. He always wears a sullen look. Sitting behind his steering wheel, he smokes bidis all the time.

'You must give me a guarantee that he won't do anything stupid again,' I tell Aisha at our next meeting. 'Otherwise, the police won't listen to me. There is every probability that, next time, I will land up in my grave.'

'You think I am in a position to give you some kind of guarantee?'

'Then what do you want? That I should let him ambush me and in return I must defend him in a court of law?'

'He won't do anything rash again.'

'How can you say that?'

'I am his mother.'

'Really!' I look at her with derision. 'A murderer's mother.'

She has no words. Seated in her chair quiet and still, she stares at me vacantly. Then she turns her head and looks out of the window.

'I am sorry.' I get up. 'You have no idea how unbearable the headaches become sometimes. Doctors say I will take time to be normal again, or maybe I might spend the rest of my life with this pain in my head.'

'I am so sorry for you. Why don't you go to Kolkata and consult some good neurosurgeon? I am ready to bear a part of the expenses.'

'Thanks for your advice. I was expecting this generosity from you,' I reply. 'You know that money isn't an issue with me. I have so much land and inheritance that I can live my life without doing anything. But is that possible for me? I come from a family of lawyers; we have made our reputation in the corridors of law. But your son's deeds have made me so weak that I can't sit in the courtroom for too long.' What I don't tell her is that I have absolutely no interest in another city apart from my own. In a way, I am living the life of a snail whose shell is this city.

'I apologize on behalf of Nadir.'

'Very well.' I smile. 'Can you give me any guarantee?'

Aisha remains silent. I haven't fully recovered from scoring a victory on her when she nods and says, 'If he ever does something like this again, I am going to strangle him with my own bare hands.'

There is enough time before the prosecution case starts. All this while, I have been seeing the accused whenever they are brought to the court. They are Aisha's relatives from her in-laws' side. I remember sending some of them to prison in earlier cases, though for a short duration. Every day, Aisha's son has to stand up in the deck in the company of the other accused. Before the appeal hearing of the bail, and for the period when he was in judicial custody, I had struck an understanding with the jail superintendent that he is not brought to the court in handcuffs and ropes. I had seen to it also that he did not fall into the hands of hardened criminals who never miss a chance to sexually exploit young boys. Now that he is out of prison, his face remains blank. He doesn't look at anyone. I am slowly regaining my strength, although I still depend on a walking stick. When they are brought into the cage, all the five accused stand unconcerned as if I were not present there.

'We should teach them a hard lesson,' the public prosecutor whispers in my ear. He doesn't like them. He really is my friend. During the court proceedings, I sit with him. We both ruminate over the finer points of the case. We are trying our best to make the case watertight from every possible angle. The defence has secured the services of the city's most experienced criminal lawyer. The back of his head is completely shaved, with a clump of hair left standing like brush on the front of his head. Despite professional rivalry, he and my father had a good equation. Whenever we run into each other, I try to act in the politest way possible. The moment he spots me, he also smiles back with fatherly affection. Every time I see him, I put my hand on my chest and respectfully bow. But I know, no matter how pleasant our personal relationship is, he will leave no stone unturned to defend his client.

'Why are you trying to save the boy's neck?' Kaku asks me one day. 'You know this will weaken the entire case. On the other hand, you are so eager to make an example of the other accused.'

'The public prosecutor agrees with you.'

'Then?'

'I am helpless.' I shrug. 'Thankfully, we have found some eyewitnesses. Some people who were on their way back from the booze den. They had not shown up in the beginning. But the police have dug them up. As eyewitnesses, they are a boon to the case.'

'It was completely dark at that time. And what do you think, these tipplers are any good as witnesses? Nobody is going to take them seriously. In the dock, they will cancel out one another's statements.'

'The investigating officer has, in his report, removed the fact of them being under the influence of liquor. As to the darkness, we will bring the sun back on the horizon. It is a matter of a few minutes only. And who will remember what the weather was that day? Maybe we will erect one or two facility poles on the sand right at the crime scene, hanging a bulb or two on them. That is not a big deal.'

I smile and look triumphantly at Kaku. 'We lawyers do that always. I think the public prosecutor will agree with me on this point.'

'I don't trust that man. He is a fraud. Maybe he is already on their payroll.'

'Don't worry, I have warned him. I know him inside out. He is on my radar all the time. I have kept an eye on everything he's doing. I will destroy him if he tries to mess up things. The Bar Association isn't very happy with this attack on a lawyer, and he knows that very well. Anyway, we are good friends.'

'What can one say to such a friendship? He is a political person.'

'What isn't political nowadays? Believe me, he has a lot of weaknesses.'

Before the start of the proceedings, the charge sheet is finalized. The public prosecutor has accused Aisha's son of being present at the crime scene but nothing beyond that. The charges levelled against the others are very serious in nature. A lot of evidence was there confirming their motivation. All the case details of Aisha's property have been handed over to the hon'ble court. Meanwhile, the high court has rejected their bail appeal. The hon'ble court is aware that the Bar Association has not taken the attack on a lawyer lightly.

The criminal case is to start next week. It has been assigned to a fast-track court. It's summer, and mosquitoes are everywhere. The river is completely dried up. People have started crossing it on bicycles and motorbikes. I don't cross the river on foot. I openly go to Aisha's place by car. We spend time together. She takes good care of me. Just a small push, and she will fall right into bed. But this is precisely the reason why my carnal desire for her has cooled off. I keep drinking tea. She goes out of the room to take care of some domestic chore. I discover that of late she has been wearing low-cut *kurti*s that reveal her ample bosom. She has got herself a new salwar kameez. They are stitched too tight for her. The contours of her hips and forearms have become very eloquent.

'Is it some kind of payoff?' One day I accuse her openly. 'I don't like it. I am trying my level best to save Nadir from conviction. You need not demean yourself.'

'You are wrong,' she says as she covers the exposed parts of her breasts with her dupatta. 'Are you still ready to marry me?'

'I will wait till the case is over... You are such a cunning woman,' I smile. 'You can't fool me. There is something else brewing in your mind.'

'Believe me, I am not trying to deceive you. You are wrong.'

'You always do it,' I reply. 'You think you will balance up the matter with your body? What are you? A mother of three children! One of them already a man.'

'What do you want?'

'I want you to stop flirting with me. This will not take you anywhere,' I say. 'When I have vowed to save Nadir, there is no need for anything else. Despite all these unpleasant things, there is a soft corner for you in my heart.'

She remains silent.

The deposition of witnesses drags on for a full twenty days. I have tutored the sham witnesses long before they are passed on to the public prosecutor. The defence lawyer knows that all the witnesses are fake. It was pitch-dark, and only a fistful of people saw some kind of mayhem on the water. That was all. They were not only in an inebriated condition, but they were also very far from the place to see things clearly. But the defence lawyer has a problem. This case involves an attack on a lawyer. The other lawyers are breathing down the neck of the public prosecutor. The entire system consciously or unconsciously wants the accused to be pushed behind bars.

The witnesses come one by one to the witness box. Meanwhile, the test identification parade has been completed, and the so-called eyewitnesses were able to recognize all the five accused without any hitch. The fact is, the public prosecutor, by taking the prison superintendent into confidence, had not only supplied the fake eyewitnesses with photographs of the accused, but we had also made sure that they came across one another, making the fake witnesses visit the jail now and then. The defence lawyer is very diligent, but unfortunately, all our witnesses bulldoze our plans. As I go through the details of the case, it dawns upon me that out of those five in jail, only three had attacked me, and they were all hired goons. They had no intention of killing me. But the rest can't really be called innocent. It's possible that they had only arranged the money, and that's why they were as guilty in the eye of law as the others. The goons have been caught. Two of them are drug addicts and one a hardened criminal, who is their leader.

Nadir's relatives had coughed up their names after the police had used the third degree.

The defence lawyer lines up several witnesses. He manages one or two alibis, too, but the witnesses turn out to be so weak that the defence lawyer has no other option but to declare them hostile. An alibi is a double-edged sword. If it fails its purpose, it boomerangs on the accused.

The cross-examination of the witnesses on both sides is finished. The doctor from the hospital sketches out my wounds in graphic detail, along with an analysis of the X-ray reports. They have a soft corner for me. We often see each other in the course of court cases. In every profession, in the course of doing one's duty, there comes a stage when a man emerging from the mire of dishonesty and bribery follows his herd instinct, which is nothing but a kind of self-defence. For them, the time has come today.

The dates for arguments have been fixed. The public prosecutor is a complete idiot in this matter. His English is very poor. He is more comfortable in the local Bengali. Thanks to his very weak and unsure arguments in Bengali, we defence lawyers often win cases that we would have lost otherwise. I spend several sleepless nights going through the deposition of the witnesses. I try to brighten up the dim corners of his mind over the phone or sitting face to face. This public prosecutor is a born idiot. He is merely surviving on political patronage. He doesn't understand most of what I say. I get fed up and write down the entire argument so that he can memorize it. Here, like most idiots, he has a really sharp memory.

He looks very nervous on the day of arguments. Maybe I have been too harsh with him. He somehow manages to vomit out the argument that he had learnt by rote. I keep staring at him in disappointment. The hon'ble judge is losing his patience at the manner he is arguing in the court. He interrupts every time the public prosecutor emphasizes a point. The defence lawyer is all smiles. The hon'ble judge has made his job easier for him. He is fully prepared for today's argument. This is his strongest area. His English is amazing. He has been defending murder cases all his life. And although the present case was giving him headaches because of a lack of proper witnesses, he presents a long-winded, heartfelt argument. His booming voice bounces off the thick walls and ceiling of the courthouse, echoing across the room, even shaking the iron bars of the accused dock, as if it will blast the cage into a thousand tiny pieces. He looks like a tempestuous river that refuses to stop. We can see all our witnesses sequentially collapse as if they were a house of cards. We almost buy the bitter fact that he will easily succeed in demolishing the whole prosecution case when a miracle takes place. His own success boomerangs on him. That forceful argument leaves an opposite effect on the esteemed hon'ble judge. The old lawyer doesn't realize this. He is like a railway engine running full steam on its tracks, when lo, the engine derails.

'Milord, I assure you, this entire incident took place in pitch-darkness when it was impossible for someone to recognize a man. All the prosecution witnesses have come up with different stories, contradicting each other's versions, as I have already pointed out in detail. And they are all habitual drinkers, a few of whom had even turned up in the court in an inebriated condition. They are all fake witnesses who have denigrated the prestige of the court. In fact, the court should take some suo moto action against these fake witnesses so that the sanctity of law can be upheld.'

'What does our respected defence lawyer suggest...' the judge bends on his table to such an extent that blood starts throbbing in his cheeks. '...that this a completely cooked-up story?'

'The case is not just cooked up, the entire attack has been stage-managed to defeat my clients in property cases.'

'This must be the first case in the history of a court when a lawyer would put his own life at risk in order to win a property case, even going so far as to stage-manage an attack on himself.' The defence lawyer realizes his mistake. But it is too late by now. Perhaps, instead of refuting the charges completely, it would have been better if he had changed the direction of the case. The public prosecutor whispers in my ear, 'The old geezer is finished! He was making such a bold show of his English vocabulary.'

'Say his name with respect!' I shoot back with annoyance. 'He is a very senior lawyer.'

'I am sorry.' He gets nervous and puts his hand on his chest, bowing reverently before the defence lawyer. There is fear in his eyes.

I congratulate the defence lawyer after he wraps up his argument. He looks worried. Defending the accused too vehemently in a murder case sometimes backfires. The esteemed hon'ble judge feels very bad about it, as if someone is pushing him to a verdict, holding him by the scruff of his neck. It's necessary for a lawyer to understand the psychological fine print and act accordingly within the accepted bounds of the law. While shaking my hand, the defence lawyer peers into my eyes. He is completely exhausted after such a long argument. His juniors have expressions of panic plastered on their faces.

We come out of the courtroom. Kaku is on his mat, dragging on his bidi. He immediately throws his bidi away and stands up to say namaskar to the defence lawyer. He is scratching his right ear as if he is ashamed of something. The senior lawyer chuckles and walks away to the veranda, his juniors in tow.

'We will win this case!' Kaku says confidently. It is difficult for him to hide his excitement.

'Are you taking opium with your bidi, Kaku?' I reply. 'He has just come out after delivering his best argument. This idiot of a public prosecutor has fucked up the entire case. Maybe I shouldn't have written down the argument and given it to him. I don't know if the judge has got wind of it.'

'No, no,' Kaku says. 'I have seen hundreds of lawyers all my life. I see defeat in his eyes, stark defeat. I can sign on it if you want!'

'We will see to that.' I take my iron chair. I am so tired. Let it be as he predicts!

It indeed turns out that way. All the five accused are sentenced to jail, each of the hired goons seven years of rigorous imprisonment, and the other two, two years of imprisonment with hard labour, and of course, with additional fines. Nadir and one of his relatives, who was not directly involved in the attack and had simply acted as a link between Nadir and the others, are acquitted of all the charges as there was a lack of proper evidence (and because I had sabotaged the case in favour of Nadir, harassing the prosecutor, which had also inadvertently helped Nadir's relative). It's Friday, 3 p.m. The shadows are getting longer. The sessions judge peers from behind his thick glasses and reads out the last page of his seventy-page judgement. The accused are asked the same routine questions. They are given the opportunity to say something in their defence or remain silent, and then, the sessions judge dictates the sentence to his stenographer. Draped in her shawl, Aisha is in a rear bench. There is a look of gratitude in her eyes. I ignore her and exit the room. The public prosecutor is overjoyed at his victory. His cheeks are flushed. He is giving his statement to the representatives of some local newspapers.

These are those one-page tabloids that look more like pamphlets than newspapers. The matter had gained the status of a high-profile case as it involved an attack on a lawyer. The handcuffs and shackles have been tightened on the convicts. The police van is being brought to take them to jail. Nadir is with his mother. Their heads bent low, they walk far apart in the opposite direction, where there are rows of small courtrooms, all wearing an empty and desolate look. Nadir's face is blank. He doesn't look at anyone. I know that the mother and son are not on talking terms since the day the case started.

The public prosecutor comes to me. The court is off for the next two days. He wants to celebrate his victory in the club. He has an expensive bottle of Scotch, which his brother-in-law, an army colonel, has smuggled to him. 'No.' I behave with him like a stranger. 'I have to attend to a lot of important matters.' He pulls his robe in disappointment and walks away, holding his books and files in his armpit. Outside, behind the trees, the sun looks tired and worn out. The court's building, its lower verandas and upper corridors are all empty, the shadows are deepening everywhere, the racket of birds is getting louder. Most of the people who come here hail from the countryside, where murder, beatings and disputes for land and inheritance are an everyday phenomenon. Long before sunset, people want to return to their villages on motorcycles or riding buses or bullock carts, or they cover the distance walking barefoot. These small villages are nothing but nests of cobras. I can say that based on my interactions with the people whom I defend. We people who live in cities are leading a safe life in comparison to them, thanks to electric lights and overcrowded streets and markets.

The holidays are over, but I have stopped going to the court. All my cases have been adjourned. The sessions judge has gone off on a long vacation. Both my windows are open. The sunlight is strong outside. Everything shudders in the breeze; even the monsoon clouds are being scattered in the sky. Birds are drying their wings on tree branches. Loaded down by paperweights, the papers are sputtering on the table in the light of the table lamp, as if trying to be free. Kaku returns before sunset. There are some clients with him. I call Kaku inside my chamber.

'Kaku, I am tired. Please handle these people.'

'Don't worry. They don't concern you. I have called them for something else. But a boy is waiting for you; he calls himself Iftikhar. He has a letter for you that he wants to deliver personally. Do you mind seeing him?'

'Send him in.'

After a few minutes, someone lifts the curtain. Iftikhar stands at the doorway.

'As-salaam alaykum!' he says, and stepping forward, places a white envelope on the table. He moves back again and stands near the door. For some seconds, I keep looking at his face. His eyes have the same aura of sadness that I had seen there in our first meeting. I pick up the envelope and turn it over to figure out what it is. There is no name on it. The envelope is thick.

'Sit down.' I lift my finger and gesture Iftikhar to take a chair without darting a glance at him.

He occupies a chair in the last row and sits there most respectfully. As I examine the envelope, he speaks up. 'Would you like to read it all by yourself?'

'Why are you saying that?' I put the envelope on the table.

'He hadn't given me any instructions, but I think he wanted me to bring it to you. I have put the letter in the envelope,' Iftikhar says, lowering his face. 'He is no longer with us.'

The room is quiet. The tick-tock of the wall clock becomes prominent. 'Was there an accident?' I pick up the envelope reluctantly.

'No. He had been sick for a long time.'

'I am sorry to hear that. The last time I saw him, he was a perfectly healthy man. Maybe it's hard to say anything with certainty about old people.' I cut open the envelope with scissors and take out the letter. It has several pages, but it has neither the name of the addressee nor the signature of the author. The date is written by a different pen. I lift my head and look at Iftikhar. 'Should I read it? I don't see my name on it. Is it okay for me to go through it? It's a long letter.'

'It's his last letter. I have no knowledge of any other letter that he wrote.'

'Will you wait for me in the veranda, just for a few minutes?'

'Maybe I should go.'

'No,' I say. 'I might need you. Don't worry; it won't take long. This is a bit strange for me.'

After he goes out, I turn over the pages serially. They are tied together only by a pin, with no serial number on them. If they separate and mix up, it will be very difficult to organize them. I staple the pages and, picking up a pen, write serial numbers on them. This is so surprising. I am reading someone's letter in Urdu after so many years. The old man's writing is astonishingly good, but as I had told Iftikhar, it contains neither the name nor the title of the addressee, nor the signature of the author. I drag my chair to the window and slide the curtains to one side, stuffing their corners into the crannies. I want to read the letter in natural light, whatever may be the reason.

I hope the news of my death has reached you by now. You may wonder – what it was that compelled me to choose you of all people to address this suicide note to. I could have addressed this note to the police for all that I care, but until you read it to the last letter, you won't be able to fathom my purpose. I want you to read this letter to the end before you arrive at any conclusion.

When I heard about the attack on you, I was a little surprised. I dug around in my own way, and working on the details of the attack, concluded that it was not something that wasn't imminent. Rather, it was surprising that as an experienced lawyer, you overlooked it. Perhaps no matter how intelligent we are, we prove idiots when it comes to our personal matters.

Maybe I shouldn't poke my nose into your personal life.

Now, whenever I think about our first meeting, I wonder why it was that our entire conversation would invariably come around to Payal, and thereafter, it would be impossible for us to leave the topic. It was not that cats carried no significance in my life. But the type of life I had been living had no room for such a hobby. In the truest sense of the word, I was myself no less than an animal who would ever care how many lives he had knowingly or unknowingly destroyed. But this is a strange phenomenon. The more a human being feels pleasure in causing agony to others, the more his life becomes gloomy in the same proportion. No wonder that something similar happened to me. And no wonder that by the end of my service, my colleagues had started to see me in a different light.

I know how surprised you were when you came to my house for the last time and found the cats confined unjustly in the cages. And why would you not be surprised? Cats aren't creatures that you can put in cages. To be honest, I myself don't know what compelled me to do that. I don't know what led me to buy my first cage. Or how the cages and cats inside them start to grow in number to such an extent that it became difficult for me to manage them. Perhaps I had lost my mind after the incident with Payal, or maybe I was taking revenge, or perhaps I had developed an infatuation for the cats as if I were a child who, in order to hide his favourite toy from the greedy eyes of the world, would not stop short of breaking it into pieces, sometimes out of mere carelessness and sometimes to make sure that no one ends up owning it, like that child who had done the beastly thing with my Payal. But as you must have discovered (and I am sure that you must have done that), I had left no stone unturned to keep the room sterilized for them. Not only that, I had also taken full care of their food, in which Iftikhar helped me a lot. In fact, for my convenience, he would go so far as to give the cats all sorts of names, though this did not stop me from mixing them up. Maybe I was simply trying to fill the void that the loss of Payal had left in my life, going so far as to buy the very house where I had been living so that I could lead my own life without being accountable to anyone. Now I could do all sorts of things that the tenants weren't allowed to do, including putting cats in cages. Will you believe me if I tell you that by doing this, I felt as if I had finally sort of fulfilled the purpose of my life? Sometimes, I would let a cat out of its cage, and after putting a collar around its neck, take it for a stroll by the river. I wish you could have seen me at those times, how haughty I would become. I searched for you everywhere, but as I discovered later on, you were lost in a world of your own. You had no time to loaf around the riverbank. And so, the days went by, and I eventually forgot you, and then, one day, all of a sudden, I heard about the news of your attack, which had spread in the city like wildfire. I was eager to see you, but every time I made a plan to come to your place, that sentence of yours would stop me – that everything has its own special place. You were not wrong. You wouldn't have liked me to come to your chamber. You might not remember this sentence of yours. We generally forget things that are of no relevance to us. Though at the time I hadn't understood a word of it, now I know what great wisdom there was in the sentence. You were right; we perhaps wouldn't have been able to make ourselves understandable to each other if it were not for this riverbank. Take it from me that if we remove this river, nothing will remain between us. So, I was telling you about my cats, which were increasing in number every day. In fact, more than three dozen cats had made their habitat in my house. They would sometimes start fighting with one another for no apparent reason, or perhaps they had a reason of their own, which no human being can decipher. But since they were shut in the cages, they had no option but to rattle the bars or to scratch them with their nails. Every time I would come into the room to find out what that racket was about, they would become quiet. Perhaps they might have had a feeling in their bones that I had brought something to eat or anticipate that it was a lucky day for one of them to have a stroll by the river. My tenants were planning to complain against me, which I could see on their faces, but whom would they complain to? I was their landlord. So, people slowly got used to my cats, to their racket, to the stench that lingered in the air despite all my efforts at cleanliness. In fact, I had started to feel that the cats were also getting used to living inside cages because the fights between them had become few and far between. So, you can understand what I am driving at right now. My life was going pretty well with the cats. They had become my universe; there was no doubt about that.

But one day, it so happened that I opened all the cages and set the cats free, each and every one of them. They disappeared into the neighbourhood through the windows or doors that I had kept wide open. This action of mine may confound you – in the first place, there was no logic in putting them in the cages, and then, for no reason, I had set them free? Really, why would I do that? Had I had an epiphany that I had unjustly put the cats in the cages? Had I done this at the suggestion of some doctor who might have instilled a fear of infection in me? Or the burden of upkeep had become too much for me? What I am about to tell you is related to a specific point. Once that point is clear, it will be easier for you to know the reason that compelled me to write this last letter to you.

You have seen my house. You must have also seen that as a tenant, I had been living in the same room for the last twenty years, but as a landlord, I now had the luxury of two rooms (out of which one was reserved for the cats), one veranda, one kitchen and one bathroom. What more did I need? I had all along been living a full life. I would draw my pension from the bank, and as landlord, I would see to it that the tenants paid their rent on time. I would pay my income tax regularly, taking into calculation all my fixed deposits, and every day, I would take out one of my cats to the riverbank, putting a collar on its neck. Everything was going along fine when one day, something weird happened.

I can't forget that particular day throughout my life. On that day, a new chapter opened in my life. It had rained a little the previous night. The sky was dark with clouds. I was trying to fall asleep after eating rotis that had been brought by Iftikhar when I heard some whispering in the feline room, as if people were talking in low voices. I woke up, and after switching on the lights, focused on the whispers for a while, and then getting out of bed, tiptoed to their door, which was wide open. I realised that the whispering had stopped of its own accord before I could switch on the light. Perhaps whoever it was had heard my footsteps. With the light coming on, I found that all the cats, be they in sitting or standing positions, were still in their cages, staring at me in unison. I could not understand where that sound was coming from. I switched off the bulb and returned to my room. I thought maybe I had misheard it. Perhaps I had mistook the sounds of the cats rubbing their bodies against the cages. I turned my face to the wall and tried to take a nap. A full hour slipped by. I tried to apply all the tricks that were at my disposal, but sleep eluded me. Soon, a cool wind started to blow in from the window, and my eyelids became heavy. I sunk deeper and deeper into darkness. I had kind of fallen sound asleep when I heard the whispering again. It was coming again from the feline room. This time, it felt like it was floating in from my dreamscape. The sound gradually became louder. I woke up. I never sleep like a log. Maybe it's because I had once been a police inspector, or maybe old people always have forty winks. I got off my bed and, after entering the other room, switched on the bulb. The voices stopped immediately. The cats were cowering in their cages, staring at me blankly. In fact, some of them were acting as if they were not there. I once again switched off the lights and returned to my room. This time, I bolted my door, but all my attention was focused on the other room. A long time elapsed. This time, there was no sound from anywhere. I can't remember when it was that I fell asleep again or how much time lapsed. In my sleep, I was hearing all sorts of voices. At last, I woke up. The *azan* was going on in a distant mosque. A loud parley was in progress in the cats' room. I tiptoed to the door and put my ear to it.

There were voices in the other room. Men, women and children, they were all taking part in it. But these were not voices that you can attribute to human beings.

'I still insist that we can organize an attack on him,' a hoarse voice raised its pitch. 'All we need to do is open one cage. Thereafter, it would be easier to open the rest.'

Whoever it was, he was not wrong because the cages were just shut from the outside, the latches merely pushed inside the slot.

'You can't compel us to rebel like this,' a feminine voice spoke up, as if she was losing her patience. 'He takes such good care of us.'

'Are you happy with this life of imprisonment?' The hoarse voice rose again. 'Do you want to lead the rest of your life in a cage? Are we made for this life of bondage?'

My god! My chest started to shake. Is it possible that these cats were having some kind of conference like human beings? I couldn't control myself. Entering the room, I groped for the switchboard and flicked on the light.

The cats were awake in their cages. There seemed to be a lot of commotion going on among them. They had sensed my presence, but it took them a while to become still. They were all on their hind legs, staring blankly at me. I studied each individual cage. The eyeballs of almost all the cats were aflame, reflecting an alien look, as if I had breached their privacy.

'Time for a nap!' I said, and picking up a stick, I rattled it across the bars of cages. 'Is there really some kind of parliamentary session going on?'

A few cats quietly cast a sidelong glance at me, and then, one by one, they all froze in their places. Some had closed their eyes, and after covering their faces with their paws, as if they were ashamed of their behaviour, they tried to establish some kind of secret contact with the other cats. They were trying their best to avoid my gaze. Finally, I switched off the bulb and returned to my room. The next night, I could not sleep a wink till it was dawn. There was dead silence in the adjoining room, too. It was as silent as a graveyard.

Several days passed after that incident. There was no commotion in the adjoining room. I tried to convince myself that it must have been my delusion. Maybe I was getting old, and my ears had started ringing with voices. The cats have overpowered my senses way too much. But then, one night, I woke up to discover that a heated argument was going on in the adjacent room, and this time, it looked like all the cats were participating in this mayhem. I entered the room and quickly switched on the bulb. A clamour was going on inside the cages. The eyes of almost all the cats were burning. The corners of their mouths were drooling. Most of the cats were on their hind legs, and resting their claws on the bars, they looked like had lost their minds.

'What are you up to behind my back?' I rattled the bars again and said mockingly. The cats were falling pell-mell to the rear wall of the cages or crouching down on the floor, they were moving their heads and shoulders. 'If you were having some kind of private conversation that involves me, which I am sure you were doing, I am at your disposal.' For a long time, I paced up and down in the room. My eyes were shooting fire at the cages. The cats looked abashed. Some of them had even hidden their faces behind their paws. Finally,

I returned to my room. I thought, *Maybe I have become too sensitive with them.* That night, I could not sleep a wink. But then, it became a routine thing. I would hear their voices every night. At midnight, standing in the dark by the door, I would try to understand their jabbering. I would always be a subject in their discussions. They would talk about their freedom, but it looked like they were not united in their opinions, as if they had split into two groups. And as always happens in such cases, one group was all for freedom and was willing to pay any price for that, while the other group seemed perfectly content with the way things were. They were satisfied with the supply of food and water, or perhaps they weren't really convinced that freedom would come so easily to them, and they didn't want to risk their neck on it. But whenever I would enter the room, absolute silence would prevail there. It was no use switching on the bulb.

'Listen,' one day I announced as I entered the room and switched on the light, 'why don't you have a man-to-man talk with me? I am the one you want. Please spit out whatever is on your mind?' But the cats kept staring. Perhaps they had no confidence in me. All I was able to elicit from them was a meow or two or some growls. In this way, the days passed by. I would remain awake the whole night, and when at daytime if I put a collar on a cat and set out for a stroll by the river, it was weird to feel that these were the same cats who would talk like human beings at night, hatching some sort of conspiracy against me. Finally, one day, I couldn't control myself and hurled a lot of invectives on them. I blamed them for being a thankless lot, giving credence to the proverb that all they cared about was their self-interest.

The cats kept listening to me attentively, but this time, there was no reaction. Then one night, something spooky happened. I found that all the cats had become mum. After several nights of this hush, in fact, after several weeks, it dawned on me that their silence was so solid it was impossible to break through it. I must admit that I felt terrified by their silence. So, one day, unable to take it any more, I entered their room to have a final talk.

'I think you guys have something to tell me?' I said. 'This is the right time to have a chat. You can blurt out whatever is going on in your mind.'

The cats gaped at me. That day, even their tails were not moving.

'All right then…' I said. 'You guys can't hold me responsible for the decision I am going to take. To be honest, I have tried my level best to keep you happy. You can't blame me that I was not sincere with you. Maybe I was wrong. I should have known that freedom is a precious thing not only for human beings but also for animals. Anyway, enough is enough, I am sick of your jabbering. Maybe I was wrong. Maybe I shouldn't have put you in these cages. So, my friends, farewell! You guys are free to go back to your feline world. This is my last night with you.'

And although it was midnight, I opened all the doors

and windows of my house, as well as all the cage doors. Most of the cats continued to sit in their cages even though the doors and windows were invitingly open, or just came out of their cages to stroll around the room. Some cats were taking rounds, keeping an eye on me, as if trying to comprehend my intentions. In fact, several cats chose a specific corner to hunker down on the floor, allowing themselves to be lulled into a deep sleep. All night long, I sat amongst them on a stool, drinking tea or holding a half-asleep cat in my lap, caressing its dull coat. And then, gradually, the cages started to become empty. Most of the cats were still asleep on the floor. Others were walking up and down in the room or staring at me. They were twisting their tails in a weird fashion, or they were stretching out on the floor as if trying to feel the freedom in their bones. It looked like this freedom was something physical in substance that they could touch or feel or figure out to make sure that something like that existed in the world. I thought maybe I had broken a kind of psychological barrier for them. So, I left them to their devices and went to bed. When I came back, I found that the room was half-empty. Whatever cats remained were disappearing one by one through the doors and windows. This exodus would stop occasionally, and things would come to a standstill and then start all over again. I sat on a chair and kept a vigil on them. It took an incredibly long time for the last cat to reach the window. The sky had become clear when I saw its silhouette on the windowsill. It was a brown cat with black circles in its eyes. It turned around and looked at me, even as half of its body was outside the iron bars, whereas the other half was inside with its tail hanging on the wall. At last, squiggling its ears, it let out a faint meow, and after taking a swift jump, vanished into the alley.

I was extremely tired. I closed all the doors and windows and slumped on my bed like a corpse. I was feeling so lonely. For the first time in my life, it looked like I had no one in the world. My tears flooded my cheeks, soaking the pillow. Soon, drowsiness took hold of me. After a long time, I enjoyed a sound sleep.

The next day when Iftikhar discovered that all the cages were empty, he was flabbergasted. 'Where did the cats go?' he enquired of me.

'Where they had come from.' I tried to crack a smile. I had just woken up and was feeling very refreshed. The sun was at mid-sky, leaving in its wake a shiny day. It wasn't as if I could now rein in my emotions as far as the cats were concerned, I had again become the same cruel, cold-hearted man that I used to be. As proof of the proverbial sour grapes, I was thinking that cats in general are a mere nuisance. Being unfaithful by nature, their presence or absence does not mean anything to us. Maybe I had only that face to bring to the world. I told Iftikhar, 'I have set them free.'

'But why?'

'Because they hate being in cages.'

'Who told you this?' Iftikhar was staring into the empty

prisons, whose teeny doors were dangling outside, as if pointing out the direction the cats had taken to disappear. 'Did we not take good care of them?'

'You can't understand this because you have never had to live inside a cage. Now your only task is either to throw out all these dirty cages or sell them in the market and make some money.'

I didn't tell Iftikhar about the debate that had gone on in the parliament of cats.

Iftikhar tied up all the cages with a rope and took them away, but he continued to bring all sorts of cats. God knows how he caught hold of them. To entice me, he would turn up with rare breeds. Sometimes, it would be a Siamese cat with a triangular head, which would be white, but her ears would be dark inside. The absolutely green cat of Thailand and cats with small heads, long legs and bright spots on their coat as if they were miniature cheetahs. Once he went so far as to appear with a Persian cat, who was quite big. Iftikhar would enlighten me with all the necessary details as if he were an expert salesman who had information about his commodity at his fingertips. I was shocked at his wealth of knowledge. The sheer variety of cats would baffle me. But I was more amazed that these cats were thriving in such large numbers in a small city. How on earth was he catching hold of them? Then I thought that once upon a time the Britishers had ruled over this swath of land; maybe these cats were the offspring of the cats that had been left behind by their wives and women, who had somehow been able to maintain the purity of their race. I was aware that over a period of time, as a result of intermingling with local cats, every species is bound to lose its identity, transmuting its breed in the bargain. I had heard that when the Britishers had sent their prisoners for the first time to Australia, they had also sent a pair of rabbits with them, who bred so fast in that continent that they are now several million in number there. This may be the case here. After all, cats aren't any less smart when it comes to replicating themselves. Be that as it may, now I wasn't ready for any kind of cat, whatever its breed. All I had found from them was bitterness. I now wanted to sleep peacefully. The tenants, too, were relieved. One of them had come in person to thank me. I had failed only Iftikhar. He was feeling so bad about the cats. Instead of selling the cages, he has kept them in his courtyard, and now he is rearing guinea pigs therein. He might even be rearing cats in them, or his family might have found other uses for the cages. I wouldn't have minded if he had earned some money by selling them off, but I could see that he was still caught up in some idiotic hope. Let me tell you one thing about that child. There is a strange refinement in his character. If you ever went to his house and saw the chaos there, or the kind of life his family leads, you would be surprised how Iftikhar has turned out such a boy. Perhaps the proverb, 'A lotus blooms in mud,' finds proof in him.

A month went by after that incident. My life was going on smoothly; I was content with my secluded life. I would pass most of my time strolling about the river. I had again started taking a few pegs of drink (which I had given up on my doctor's advice) because it was now my only source of peace. I would ask Iftikhar to take a sip or two, but the taste was not to his liking. He would just sit with me and chuck *chanachur* into his mouth or eat salad. He had no objection to my addiction to alcohol. He would prepare my plate of *gazak* and mix my drink. Of late, I have been sending him to the market to buy my liquor. He had become a dropout in school. I tried to send him back to his class but to no avail. Perhaps the atmosphere in his house wasn't conducive to it. My life was going on as such when suddenly, one night, I woke up again to see my window lit up by a huge moon. I opened my eyes as wide as I could to discover, to my amazement, that two male cats were atop the moon, talking to each other in conspiratorial tones. This time, their voices were quite clear.

'I don't agree with you. Our coming here is a sheer mistake. This is no place for us.'

'There isn't a single cage in the room.'

'Cages can be bought any time.'

'How can you forget all his favours, all he did for us? Believe me, this man has changed.'

'Human beings never change. They change their face as per circumstances. We can't stay in this house.'

I got off my bed, and taking some hushed steps, went to the wall to switch on the bulb. I found that two cats were sitting on the floor facing each other. When I turned and looked back at the window, I couldn't see the cats there. Maybe it was my imagination that had led me to think that they were sitting on the moon. In fact, the cats on the floor were talking to each other. When they found that I was staring at them, they took giant leaps and vanished through the window into the dark courtyard. And although I tried to take a nap again after switching off the light and did, in fact, fall asleep, I had a premonition that this was a new beginning. My apprehension turned out well-founded. The cats had returned. Now I could hear them every night. They would crawl in through the window or come out of the adjoining room, descend from the roof or the staircase or sometimes even pop up from the underside of my divan. These became such routine things that they compelled me once again to keep my doors and windows closed before I went to bed. But the result of this precaution was even worse. Now they started to rattle the door or thump the window; in fact, their meows had adopted an angry tone, ending sometimes in growls. And this would go on all through the night. I would open my door, but there would be nothing except a few disappearing shadows. Thereafter, there would be a long spell of silence. But I would barely close my eyes when the sounds would start all over again. This was something so weird that any human being would have gone insane. If I left the doors and windows ajar, the cats would come in and stand in the middle of the room and start their strange conversation. If I left them shut, they would knock continuously at the doors and windows. To scare them away, I would keep a stick at the head side of my bed. Now, whenever the knocking started, I would beat the door or the window with my stick. Once in a while, I would open my door to see them disappear, scaling the boundary wall. It came to such a stage that immediately after sunset, I would get the drift of something ominous. All night long, I would wait with my lights on, keeping the doors and windows wide open. But no sooner I would doze off than they would turn up from nowhere. You may say they were playing hide-and-seek with me. Four months have gone now. I am fed up of staying up awake all night. I am fed up with my night-long vigil. I have decided to sell the house. But this will take time, and anyway, who would be interested in a house that has been completely occupied by tenants? Of late, I have not been keeping well. It is not possible for me to put up with such painful nights. What's shocking is that the cats are not visible to my tenants and neighbours. They think they are a figment of my imagination. But believe me, they come every night in flesh and blood. I don't know what motive brings them back and what urge for revenge or what kind of love draws them towards me, but they keep coming all the same. You can see the marks of their grimy paws as also scratches from their nails all over my bed, table, chairs, even on the walls. In fact, right now as I am writing this letter to you, one of them is roaring outside the window. Today, for the first time in my life when I am writing this last letter to you, I realize how miserably I have failed in my life. Perhaps to escape this fiasco, I had sought refuge in the company of cats, in utter disregard of the fact that human beings and cats have nothing in common. Today, I know that as humans beings, all we have done is impose ourselves on this earth for no reason. There is no way to prove our humanity other than packing up our things and setting off for somewhere remote in the dark universe. These cats remind me that we human beings are nothing but 'trespassers' on this earth.

The time has come. I am ready for my last journey. I will decamp any day from this world with my mortal remains. I wish we could have met before that happens. I wish this letter reaches you one day.

P.S.: I am giving this note to Iftikhar with explicit instructions that in case I suddenly give up my ghost, within a week of it, the letter should reach you. I have no qualms to admit that I have shown your house to Iftikhar. He is a smart kid; once you tell him something, it will stay with him forever. I don't know if he will take proper care of this letter because, as I have told you earlier, there is so much chaos in his house. His grandfather is an inveterate drunkard, a scoundrel to his bone. Thanks to him, his entire house reeks of effluvia. I know once I am dead, my people will not take much time to take over my house. From my experience, I have found that relatives are nothing but vultures who just wait for you to kick the bucket so that they can rip off the last piece of flesh from your body. It may so happen that this letter goes to waste or gets lost in the aftermath of my death or is entirely forgotten in the mayhem. In that situation, I am content with my fate!

But whenever I see Iftikhar, a firm belief takes hold of me that one day, this letter will reach your table. He is such an extraordinary kid.

I look up from the letter towards Iftikhar.

'This letter is dated fifteen days back. Why did you take so long to come to me?'

'He didn't give me this letter,' Iftikhar replies. 'He was severely ill. The doctors were of the opinion that he should be hospitalized as soon as possible, but he would vehemently oppose their proposal. Come what may, he was adamant to stay in the house. Gradually, his condition deteriorated. He couldn't pass urine. When he passed away, I found this letter stuffed in a pillow. I myself have written the date on it. The doctors were too busy to see me remove it.'

So he didn't have a chance to commit suicide. Nature had decreed a natural death for him!

'There is no name or address in the letter.' I turn the letter over and examine it. 'What made you bring this letter to me? How did you find out that this letter is meant for me? He might have written it for anyone.'

'I don't know. We had come to your gate several times. For hours on end, we would sit on the trunk of a fallen tree next to the ditch of the Chinese Mansion where Payal had disappeared one day. He would never enter your gate.'

'Maybe this letter is meant for some colleague of his.'

'It might be,' Iftikhar says. 'Some of his colleagues used to come to him. They had stopped coming lately. I don't even know their addresses. If this letter is not for you, please return it to me, sir.'

'No, that's not what I mean,' I take out a hundred-rupee note from my pocket and try to pass it on to him. 'No doubt, the letter was meant for me. Call me if you need more money.'

'I can't take this money,' the boy says, pulling his hands away, even though from where he is standing, he can't take the money even by extending his hand. 'I just wanted to make sure that this letter reaches the right person. Some of his relatives have already arrived. I have seen them for the first time in my life. None had dared to turn up when he was alive. Now that he is dead, they have come. They have occupied the house. They are collecting rent from the tenants. They have also started to threaten them with eviction. They are very cruel people. They regard us with suspicion. Had they received this letter, there wasn't a chance it would be delivered to you.'

'I am grateful for that,' I say. 'Will you do me one more favour?'

'Yes. Please tell me.'

'Can you take me to his grave?'

'You want to go now or later? It won't be difficult for you to recognize his grave even if I am not there.'

'Really, how's that?' Iftikhar falls silent.

'All right, we can talk on our way. Just wait for two minutes.'

When we are on our way to the graveyard, a sluggish wind blows, carrying the chirping of birds. A clear day is at its end. White clouds pass in a blue sky. There is only one graveyard for Muslims in the city, which is next to the railway line. As we open its iron gate, which is never locked, we discover that the graveyard has been overrun by undergrowth and bushes as if we are in a forest. This happens every rainy season here. There is a strange story about these bushes. Once the rainy season is over, Muslim men, women and children come from a nearby village in large numbers to chop off all the bushes and clear the graveyard of the undergrowth, though sometimes, it takes weeks to finish the job. Poor people though they are, they never accept a rupee for their labour.

'Do you come here often?' I ask Iftikhar.

'Yes, all our relatives are buried here. They were good people.'

'I know. All my people also live in this graveyard.'

Walking through the bushes, we reach the shade of an old banyan tree, where there are rows of cemented graves. This is a very old graveyard. Iftikhar stops in front of a new grave next to a tree. As I cast a look at it, I am shell-shocked, and I understand immediately what Iftikhar meant when he had said that I will recognize the grave. Several cats are sitting over it or crawling about. Some more cats are emerging from the bushes. Finding us there, some of them take a U-turn and vanish into the bushes. Gradually, all the cats scamper off, leaving the grave empty.

'These cats... have they made this grave their permanent habitat?' I look at Iftikhar in disbelief.

'Every time I come here, I find them. The gravedigger would try to chase them away, but it was useless. They would return in no time,' Iftikhar says as he raises his palms for *fatiha*. 'They keep increasing or decreasing their numbers, but I can't remember a time when this grave has been without them.'

We stay in the graveyard for ten minutes. We are returning after offering *fatiha* when we see the cats again. They are emerging from their hideouts, making a beeline for the grave.

'Are these the same cats?' I ask.

'No, I recognize them all,' Iftikhar replies. 'These are different ones.'

Chapter Four

DESPITE THE FACT THAT THE DEATH OF THE sub-inspector has shaken me to my core, I don't know why it is that on my way home, I feel a kind of lightness, as if a heavy burden has been lifted from my soul. Death... sometimes it solves a lot of problems, problems we fail to make head or tail of. It was clear from the letter that he was firmly resolved to commit suicide, but maybe his illness had disabled him. Perhaps this was good for him. To carry on a life with no purpose is like digging a hole in the earth to escape the boredom of a dark and dull sky, nurturing a silly hope in your heart that maybe one day you will emerge on the other side of the planet and see a day of bright sunshine and the chirping of birds while a wind blows through the trees, showcasing a universe where everything is all right. But spending your life in such a tunnel, standing enveloped in a darkness, besmeared in mud, and getting weaker and weaker in its miasma and stuffiness, you don't even realize that you have reached the fag end of your life because, in the dark tunnel, you not only lose track of time, but you also fail to realize what kind of metamorphosis has taken place inside you. And then, one day, you throw away the pickaxe and, falling on your knees, hold your head in your hands in utter helplessness because it suddenly dawns on you that the tunnel is not going to end, that you are standing on a spot from where you can neither go forward nor back. This is the time for you to accept the reality of the tunnel, that you are going to draw your last breath in it. He was lucky that nature helped him escape this tunnel; otherwise, god knows how long he would have spent in that place, just like billions of people who are spending their lives on this cursed planet.

Should we call this a pleasant evening when the sun is not in the sky, but it is still daylight on earth? I return to my gate. The Chinese Mansion stands vacant. Only a jaundiced light flickers in its upper floor. People are getting ready for the evening on both sides of the street. One or two fireflies emit light in the open drain. Crickets are chirping. Light falls on thorny bushes along the drains like droplets of water. Soon, the moon will gain light in the sky, which, for want of darkness hangs like a paperweight. This is very much like those human beings whom we lose sight of because we had been interacting with them all the time, and then, something occurs, and the contours of their faces become visible. Factories are a rarity in our city and its suburbs. There is never enough water in the river to sustain any kind of industry. Maybe that's the reason that there is barely any impurity in the air, except dust particles that fail to rise very high. During the monsoon, when the air is crystal clear, stars sparkle in the sky like diamonds. Sometimes, they come so close to the earth that they leave us dumbfounded. And today, the horizon is absolutely clear. This street on which our house and the Chinese Mansion stand has its origin in the city market, which, passing through our house and the Chinese Mansion, goes on to the river, where it terminates at the cremation ground. There has been a long-standing plan to build a bridge at the river. Before every election, the foundation stone is laid with a lot of pomp and mayhem. There would be highfalutin political speeches, and then, the entire matter is shelved until the next election. At some point of time in the past, this used to be the most affluent area of the city, but as happens to such places, all the prosperity of the people has gone down the drain. The present residents are the entities whose forefathers were the beneficiaries of foreign masters. The boundary walls on both sides of the road are either cracked or have collapsed, where bushes and brambles rule the roost. Perhaps people don't have enough money to pay for the upkeep of such big houses, or perhaps they are eccentrics like me. I walk all the way to the cremation ground and sit on a wall. The plaster is gone from most of the places, laying bare the bricks. There are water marks at the concrete steps. The riverbed looks like a vast desert with no end. Whenever I end up coming to this ghat, I always see a pyre or two burning on its sand. Once the cremation is over, the people break their earthen pots, as also the charpoy, and walk away along the river, vanishing into the mist. But today, the ghat is empty and desolate. There is moonlight on the sand. The sub-inspector's death is gradually sloughing off my psyche like a snake discarding its skin, but I know that one day, this incident will come hurtling back through the skies like a satellite and hit me hard at a place where I am least prepared for it. This has been happening to me always, like my father's death, which is getting bigger and bigger every year, like a magical stone which is, at the end, going to crush me under its weight, whereas this tunnel is not of my making.

After returning home, I sit in my chamber and flip through pending case files. Soon, I get fed up, and I go upstairs to my bedroom, whose human-sized windows have become dark. I doze off after my third glass of whisky. I know this night is going to be crammed with bad dreams; maybe it is this apprehension that periodically wakes me up. Sometimes, to pass water, I go to the bathroom, or an intense thirst wakes me up. Whenever I close my eyes, this or that dream will take hold of me, but every time I open them, nothing lingers in my memory. I want to forget the faces of the accused, but they refuse to go away. When the case was going on, I hadn't heard any of the accused utter a single word. The rest of the night turns out worse. Several old dreams repeat themselves. Snakes chase me. This is an old habit of theirs. They have been chasing me all my life. I walk naked through the crowd of people. I fall from the sky though there is no sign of land anywhere. Caught in the grip of an unnamed fear, my heart beats so hard that I can't breathe. I want to say something, or scream, but my voice refuses to come out of my mouth. Am I going to die? I see people. They are covering the riverbed with a shroud. It is almost morning when I see Aisha. She stands naked on the sand, with a blank look in her eyes. Colourful butterflies cover her nipples. I crawl on my knees, reach her crotch and rub my cheek on her pubic hair. She takes my head in a tight grip. I try to pull it away, but Aisha is overflowing with desire. She grasps my hair firmly, and putting huge pressure on the back of my head, tries to suffocate me. I let out a scream and wake up. The room is dark. She is now outside the windowpanes with butterflies fluttering on her nipples.

The air is quite chilly, but my entire body is drenched in sweat. My god! Am I slowly losing contact with the reality?

I hide my face in the pillow. I am afraid to close my eyes. They are filled with shards. Time gradually passes until there is light outside. I enter my bathroom and take a bath in cold water. The phone rings in my room. I know who must be calling at this early hour. I take my time under the shower. Off and on the phone rings in a monotonous tone. It rings one last time and falls silent.

I stay in my room the whole day. Kaku comes up several times with some urgent papers. He needs my signature on them, but I send him away without signing the documents. I drag my chair to the window and make myself comfortable in it. All the doors and windows of the Chinese Mansion are shut as if its residents have left it for good. I am surprised at myself. Before this, no case had ever taken hold of me in such a manner. But now, when the entire case has gone in my favour, why is it that suddenly I am feeling so guilty? An emptiness has taken hold of me, as if I have become a part of the deep silence that is spreading its wings on the earth and the skies. It is night again. I sink deep into sleep. Last night had gone very bad for me. When I wake up, my gaze falls on the glass of whisky that I had not touched. A moth is floating on its surface. I pick it up, and bringing it to the light of the lamp, cast a surprised look at it. Had the moth come flying out of my dream? Its wings are yellow with black lines making an imprint of an eye on them. I go to the balcony and pour the whisky into the basin. I cast a glance at the inner courtyard, which is cluttered with old run-down furniture. A cat emerges from the jungle of furniture and tiptoes across the veranda. Her tail is curled up. I try to remember her breed, but she looks more or less like a regular cat to me.

That day, I reach court very late. It was supposed to be a very busy day for me, but luckily, most of the cases are adjourned. Kaku handles the rest. I just sit on my iron chair and smoke cigarettes.

'It is time for you to tie the knot...' Kaku is picking up documents from the floor mat and marking them with a red pencil. He doesn't look at me as he says this. Like always, a bidi is stuck between his lips and a pencil tucked on his right ear. He has slowed down a bit after his heart attack. The doctor has advised him not to smoke, but he is in no mood to follow his instructions. '...otherwise, it will be too late.' He completes his sentence.

'I completely agree with you.' I nod, though my intention is to simply avoid the topic. After returning home, I bathe for a long time. I put on my best clothes. I always polish my shoes before I go out. I don't find Mir up to the mark when it comes to these small things.

'You have been crossing the river on foot again.' Kaku has returned from court, and like always, he has taken up his work. Seeing me on my way out, he doesn't hesitate to intervene. 'You have stopped using the car again. Why don't you take it? It just stands idle all day long. You are embroiled in a number of murder cases. Learn to protect yourself.'

I smile at him. There is nothing good in Kaku's life. If we look at things from his point of view, we are living on a dark planet. Perhaps it's his work that keeps him alive.

'I have grown up by the side of this river. A lot of trees have been felled on both sides, making the place less scary now. After the conviction, their morale is down.'

'Don't be such an optimist,' Kaku says. 'Villagers aren't that wise. Of late, you have been fighting serious criminal cases that involve village people. These rascals don't care about consequences. And on top of that, you have just sent five of their men to prison. It's not safe for you to go alone. Nazeer just sits around and passes time. God knows how he manages to sleep all day long in that small seat of the car. If you insist on taking a stroll at the riverbank, try to be home before sunset.'

Perhaps Kaku knows about my destination. He does not stop me. He has never seen my relationship with Aisha in a good light. His eyes always betray his apprehension that I am standing at the edge of a cliff, and it only requires a soft push to send me hurtling into the abyss.

'I will come back soon.' I deliberately evade him and head out towards the river. It's a pleasant day. There is a motley crowd at the riverbank. Rickshaws, bicycles and bullock carts are crossing the river. Winter is in its prime. The sun is shining right in the middle of the sky. The shadows of the trees have receded to their trunks. As I walk on the sand, I look across the water over and over again. I don't know why the other bank looks so close today. I return home.

Today the court is closed. Kaku hasn't been coming for the last two days. His phone is also silent. I sent Nripen to his home. I call Aisha and inform her that I am coming. She is overjoyed at the news. Kaku is not present to stop me. I take a brief afternoon nap and then set out towards the river. As I walk on the sand, I feel an onslaught of cold wind that usually blows here at this time of the year. A balloon peddler walks in front of me, but he is coming to the city instead of going across the river. After some time, as I look back, all I can see are his balloons fluttering in the wind amidst the people who are crossing the river. A pinwheel seller has stuck his pole in the sand, and sitting on his heels, he is pissing shamelessly in broad daylight. It's the season for the monsoon to make a comeback. The sun's orb has become dim, as if a black spider lies shrivelled and dead in its web. A sort of melancholy pervades everything. This is a very special day for me. Today, we are going to make a very important decision. Soon the river falls behind, and I emerge on the road. There is an eerie silence here. This silence is natural at this time of the day. I stop for a while on the road and stare down the slope where mud houses stand in a row ending at Aisha's three-storeyed brick building. The building looks empty and abandoned from this height. Most of its windows are shut. Descending from the slope onto the narrow dirt road, which is absolutely quiet, I pass through the mud houses and finally stand in front of Aisha's house. I rattle the iron gate, but no one responds. Perhaps Aisha and her kids are asleep. The paan shop is shut as also the bakery, where, in daytime, one can always see a few customers. I once again rattle the iron gate. This time, a window opens on the upper floor, and Aisha appears in its frame. Recognition flashes across her eyes, and she vanishes from sight. I can hear the wooden staircase creak loudly.

Aisha is at the gate. Her hair is dishevelled. We both stand silent for a long time, staring at each other. Her cheeks are flushed. Her right hand is coated in flour. Maybe she had been working in the kitchen.

'I am a little late,' I say, looking at the sky, where clouds are collecting.

'No, no. You are right on time,' she says as she cleans her

hands with the edge of her sari. 'I am cooking something special for you. You will be happy to meet Nadir. We have talked freely for the first time after that incident.' Her voice is trembling. Her cheeks are flushed with tears, though the edges of her lips are all smiles.

'Maybe I should have given you more time. I don't want to rush it.'

'You are worried for no reason. Please come in.' She opens the gate.

'There is a strange silence here,' I say.

'This happens here sometimes.' Aisha's voice is mellow. I hold her hand. She doesn't resist. 'Thank you, thank you!' she says in a low voice. I don't know what it is that she is thanking me for. I let her hand go as we climb the stairs. Her fingers are trembling. Maybe she is overflowing with sexual desire.

'Children?'

'They are downstairs, playing.'

At the first-floor landing, she switches on the light, although it is not necessary. Maybe she wants to impress on other members of her family that there is nothing unusual between us. Suddenly, I feel very close to her. I stop at the stairhead and look at her. Perhaps she has also been waiting for this moment. Her ears are beautiful. She has gold earrings on them. She is aware of the beauty of her ears because she has pulled her hair aside and arranged it in such a manner that they are clearly visible. She has used a lot of clips and pins for this purpose. The corners of her intense eyebrows are drawn upwards like swords, and on the wrinkled corners of her lips, there is a hint of a smile. She falls into my embrace, unable to hold herself back. I don't even realize that our lips have found each other so easily. She is turning savage. We enter her room in this condition, kissing each other. She then pulls away from me and opens the window curtains. The room is bathed in daylight. Birds are chirping in the ruined garden, which feels like an untimely song. It might be the result of the darkness that has descended so early from the clouds. Aisha stands by the window. Standing behind her, I look outside into the world, where the wind has woken up. Both her younger children are in the garden, playing with their maid. Nadir is in their private graveyard, standing between two graves.

'Are those the graves of Nadir's grandparents?'

'No, his grandfather and father are buried in those graves. His grandmother had passed away long before the land was bought for this purpose. The other graves belong to our relatives. They come here on and off to bury their dead. There are also graves of our acquaintances who have built their houses nearby. In a way, it's no longer a private graveyard.'

She might be right because the graveyard has no boundary wall of its own other than the garden wall, which stands on one of its sides. At the periphery of the graves, there is a clean water drain. This drain belongs to the irrigation department. A nozzle of a pump is spewing water into the field where mustard plants stand but haven't flowered yet. Thick smoke is coming out of the exhaust pipe of the pump, dissolving into the thin air.

'What is he doing there?' I point at Nadir, and moving Aisha away, thrust my hands outside the window. 'Hey, boy,' I cry out in a loud voice. 'Why don't you come upstairs? I want to have a talk with you.'

Nadir looks up, and turning around, enters the garden. After closing the gate from inside, he pulls the latch into its slot.

'He was the absolute favourite of his grandpa. His father and grandfather died within a month of each other.'

'The eldest son of a house carries a huge psychological burden,' I say, although I don't know what I mean by that. After a while, I see Nadir at the door. I had never looked at him so closely during the entire court proceedings. He has become quite tall. He also looks somewhat confident. He doesn't come inside but stands at the door with his hand on the door frame.

'Come in,' I say. He comes inside and sits on the three-legged chair in front of the bed. He is staring straight into my eyes.

'I am going to the kitchen. I was working there before you came.'

'No, no. Stay here. I can't talk in your absence.' I sit on the bed in front of Nadir and take his right hand. 'Nadir, you have become an adult now. I think we can talk freely. Would it be wrong if I say that we should let bygones be bygones?'

Nadir shakes his head. He slowly withdraws his hand. Aisha is looking out of the window. 'You know that we love each other and want to get married. We should have told you this a long time ago.'

Nadir remains silent. 'Why don't you say something?' I take his hand again. 'You are a man now. We can't do this without your permission.'

Nadir looks at me and smiles. 'My mistake. Right from the beginning, I had no reason to be in your way.'

'Forget it, I don't hold any grudge for that. And it wasn't that easy for you to accept this relationship.'

'Mother...' Nadir stands up from his chair. 'We are going to Grandpa's place. We will be back at night. If we end up being very late, we will meet tomorrow morning.' He stops at the door and smiles at me. 'Sir, you have done so much for us. I am sure that Mother will be happy with you.'

Aisha goes downstairs with Nadir. She has to get her kids ready. The maid brings tea for me. She knows very well what the purport of my visit is – or what specific intention has brought me today. Her lips are all smiles. She might be Aisha's confidante. Aisha returns after dropping the kids at Nadir's motorcycle. The maid is in tow. 'You may rest a bit,' she tells the maid. The maid smiles and walks off. She shuts the door from outside.

'She knows what is going on between us,' I say.

'She isn't an idiot. Ever since her husband left her because she didn't bear him a baby, she has been living with us.

Although her husband has married again and has children from his second marriage, he comes to see her secretly, though we have strictly forbidden it. Maybe she herself is complicit in it. One day, Nadir caught them red-handed. He beat the man black and blue. He has stopped coming here, but I am not sure. Maybe they meet outside somewhere. We can't really be sure. She has been living here for at least ten years now. It isn't strange that she knows everything about us.'

We stand face to face when she smiles again. I hold her hand.

'I will see to it that the marriage is solemnized as early as possible, maybe someday next week.' I run my fingers through her hair with white strands visible through henna. 'It will take one or two weeks at the most. After our marriage, I want you all to come to my place and live there.'

'What about this house?'

'We will be coming here now and then. Your kids are going to have all the rights over land and inheritance.'

'I don't think Nadir will be happy with this arrangement.'

'Let's talk about it later.'

And as I kiss her, she gropes for the switchboard and flicks off the mercury light. Darkness descends in the room, from which things start to emerge gradually.

'I want to see you in light.' I take my hand to her back and pull down the zip of her blouse.

'No, no. No light,' I hear her protest in an intense voice. She takes her hands to her back and unhooks her bra. The straps come loose, and the bra hangs limply on her upper arms. Her breasts are well-formed, rather on the heavy side. They smell of sweat. The touch of my fingers awakens them; the nipples become stiff. She lets out a sigh of relief. She doesn't look like a woman who is thirty-six-years old and is nervous like a newly-wed. She takes my left hand and places it on her right nipple, massaging my fingers with hers, kneading her breasts like dough. Women are sexually more sensitive at some specific spots, and Aisha's breasts are one such place that you can tap to rouse her desire. Her nipples have hardened quite a bit. They must have felt a male touch several centuries back. Today, the snow is melting. From a frozen state, she is becoming warm water again. She is also the first woman in my life. My chest quivers as I hear her heart beating loudly. I find it hard to locate her vagina, or maybe I am rushing it too fast. Initially, she doesn't make any movement, as if she isn't concerned with this carnal quest of mine, then she sighs, takes a firm grip of my organ and guides it to her vagina. But it's quite late by then. As my organ meets her fingers, a tickling sensation is unleashed in my veins. She lets my organ go, but by then, my desire has peaked. It rises to the sky, stays there for a while, where fireworks explode among the stars, and then converges to the centre of my being. Despite all my restrain, I reach a climax, and the stream flows wave by wave, leaving me drained. The storm is over. I stand at the shore, where there is dead silence. I am ashamed of myself. In my hurry, I let her down. I somehow sit up and look at Aisha through a mist.

'I am sorry. I have messed up your bed.'

'Nothing to worry about it.' She sits up, and stifling a yawn, smiles and casts a sidelong glance at me. She has pulled the bedsheet to her crotch. Her breasts bulge down. The storm has blown over. It was only the tip of the storm that she was able to see from the shore. But she has the consolation that she is the first woman in my life. She gets down from the bed and stands naked in front of the window, staring out of it. There is a full moon in the sky. She turns. Our eyes meet in the dark.

'It's a full moon night,' she says. 'Every full moon night brings a lot of pain in my cycle. It happens to some women. I was very scared. I don't know, but I wasn't in a state to have sex.'

'Then whatever happened was for the best,' I say.

'I don't know.' She draws the curtain across the window and lies down on the bed. 'I am so scared of a full moon night.'

The clouds hang very low in the sky. The round orb of the moon, half visible behind the blurred edges of a cloud, dangles in the sky like a giant paperweight.. I put on my clothes and stand in front of the window, smoking a cigarette. Time drifts away. The garden has become dark. The moon has sunk deeper into the clouds, and it's highly unlikely that it will emerge again. Aisha is lying in bed with her eyes closed. 'Aisha,' I go closer to her and, caressing her hair, whisper into her ears. 'Time for me to go.' She doesn't answer me but hugs me tightly. In these moments when the storm is over, there is no space for any sound or movement between us. I whisper words of affection in her ears, which I myself can't hear. Even though I behaved like an idiot, after this fiasco, I want to be alone. I free myself from her clutches and start wearing my shoes.

She sits up, crossing her arms over her bare breasts, and stares blankly at me. Her eyes loom large in the darkness. After a while, she switches on the light, pulls the bed sheet off and throws it in a corner. She puts on her clothes and goes out of the room. When she returns, she is in different clothes. She has a purse, an umbrella and a small torch. In the meantime, I went to the bathroom, and after cleaning myself, I again sit on the edge of the three-legged chair. I am so tired. She pulls the curtains apart and stares out of the window as if surprised at the absence of the moon. The clouds have darkened the sky, which has almost receded from view. The wind has stopped. I put on the shoes that I had taken off before going to the bathroom and tie up my laces; this is when she suddenly turns and casts a look at me. 'What do you think? Has Nadir accepted our relationship?'

'Do you doubt it? You yourself said that both of you had an honest conversation. Anyway, it's not important now. We have crossed that bridge.'

'He has been showering so much love and attention on me. Have you ever found someone's love scary?'

'I can't say. I had always been kept away from my mother. Goats would be reared in our house to get me milk. I have no idea what maternal love is, and I don't regret having lost it because how can you lose something that you never had? But don't worry. I will send Nadir to an expensive college, somewhere far from this place. I know a lot of influential people. He will forget everything once he is in a new place in the company of new friends. The younger ones like me. I don't think I will have any trouble with them.'

'That sounds good. I have cooked some nice things for you. You will like them.'

'I think it's too late for that. The weather is getting worse. I should go. Some other time.'

She doesn't insist but expresses her desire to accompany me to the riverbank. The night is dark, the riverbed is not visible. It's so suffocating. Maybe the sand has not cooled off. We see the silhouette of a rickshaw on the rock. The rickshaw puller is nowhere. We wait for him.

'You have again crossed the river on foot. What happened to your car?'

'I like to cross the river on foot. You will have to cover thirty more miles via the dam to get here by car. It's not safe to drive back after dark. There are a few villages among the barren hillocks that are practically nests of criminals. And I also avoid my car so people don't give you a bad name. Nazeer has become too nosey about our personal matters. I think I should fire him and get a new driver.'

'He is an old employee of yours. What if the new driver turns out equally bad?'

'Maybe you are right. We can't really change the world.'

We see the rickshaw puller. After dropping off the passenger, on the way back he had gone off to the liquor den. He is extremely drunk. He takes so long to light up the lantern that at one point it looks like he has dozed off. The mixed odour of kerosene and alcohol is assaulting my nostrils. Aisha stands apart, covering her nose with her dupatta. She is focusing the torch on him. The rickshaw puller is smiling and glaring at her as he cleans his chimney with a rag. I think, after our marriage, my drinking habit is going to give me a lot of trouble.

'He is swaying so badly. He can't even stand on his feet. It is better that you wait for another rickshaw.'

'It's hard to find another one in such bad weather. Don't worry. He is drunk, but I will take care of him.'

And predictably, as the sand slowly starts to crackle under the wheels, the weather takes a turn for the worse. It starts to drizzle. The rickshaw puller gets off his saddle and pulls the canvas over my head. He pulls down the tarps up to his saddle. He covers his head in a polythene bag. Despite the darkness, he looks so hilarious in it. I lift the tarp that is hanging on my back and look back at the road above, where Aisha stands with her umbrella. She is moving her torchlight right and left, signalling her presence. Looking at her from the riverbed, she looks like a lighthouse throwing its beam from the crest of a rock. I wave goodbye. I don't know if she saw it. The light of the lantern is too faint. I last see her standing on a rock, waving her torch.

After my meal, I take a stroll on the terrace. Notwithstanding the strong gusts of wind, I am enjoying the dark sky, relishing the idea that Aisha's house is also under the same sky. I walk around for a long time. The drizzle that started when I was returning from Aisha's house stopped when I was halfway home. Thereafter, it was the wind that took over, which is still raging.

Mir appears with a torch.

'I see a storm coming. You will catch a cold.'

'I will take a few minutes,' I say, but instead of staying on the terrace, I follow him downstairs. He is right. The rain starts in a short while. He serves food in my room as the rain gains momentum. Soon, the rain transforms into a full-blown storm. After my dinner, behind closed windows, I try to read a book. The window glasses are rattling in their sashes as are the aluminium blinds. I see a streak of white light rise to the sky in which leaves and branches are swirling. I try to concentrate on my book, focusing on the words, with my blanket pulled up to my chest when suddenly, the electricity goes off. I put the book in my lap and look out of the window. Such foul weather, there is no hope of the electricity coming back soon. I hear the stomping of feet. Mir appears with a kerosene lamp, which he sets down on the table next to the head panel of the bed. His clothes and hair are wet.

'You will catch a cold.' I pick up the book from my lap and keep it on the side table.

'This rain is a real headache,' he says. 'Such a big house. It is difficult to locate everything that is lying exposed to the rain. Do you want something, some tea or coffee? I have to check and see if Jhabra is all right.'

'He must be cowering somewhere in the house, terrified of the storm. However, you had better look. Also, make sure that the library windows are properly shut, right?'

'Kaku always closes them before he leaves. But I will check them again.' He goes away.

As the storm rages outside, I look at the kerosene lamp. In his rush, Mir did not clean it properly. Its wick has taken on a weird shape, lending the flame a preternatural look. It is blackening the chimney. I lower the wick by rotating the lever. The shadows change their places. A branch that has been continually hitting a windowpane gets stuck to it, its prickly leaves shuddering. Trees must have fallen along the river. The riverside will make a good spectacle tomorrow morning. I close my eyes and try to take a nap, thinking all along about the boats sailing in the river. It turns out to be a catnap. I keep my eyes shut and lie in my bed. It's not long before the electricity comes back. I open my eyes and look at the window. Though there is light in the room, it is pitch-dark outside. Slowly, things start to take shape. The storm has abated. Through the white sheet of rain, the outlines of houses and trees are visible. The chimney of the lamp is blackened completely. I turn it off, as well as the mercury light, and try to fall asleep. First, the storm disturbed me, and now, I can't fall asleep because of the quiet in the room. For a long time, I stare with open eyes at the ceiling, where a slice of light falls from somewhere. I think of the Earth that is rotating on its axis in a dark universe. It's so surprising that, completely unconcerned about the Earth spinning like a top, we human beings wander about in search of our petty pleasures!

In the morning, the city is enveloped in melancholic weather. The rain that stopped in the wee hours has resumed, but it doesn't have the same intensity now, although clouds are gathering in the sky, draping the city in a black mourning shroud. There is a small telephone box outside my window from which innumerable wires spring out to enter my house and all the other houses in the neighbourhood. A crow has flown in from somewhere. Perched atop the box, it is cleaning its beak. Its soaked feathers are sticking to its body, and it looks stark naked. It lifts its head over and over again to look at the sky. After cleaning out its beak on the metal, it remains quiet for a while and then, with a short caw, fervently moves about on its feet on the tin box while twisting and turning its head around. I don't know when I dozed off or whether the crow was still there on the box. This time, it is a long dream in which people with pickaxes on their shoulders cross a stone bridge over and over again. I am inside a house somewhere near that bridge. This dream ends up with the ringing of the telephone. The phone might have been ringing continuously for some time. I look at the wall clock. It's 7 a.m. This means that I have barely slept for fifteen minutes. Ah, in our dreams, time changes its speed in such a bizarre way! Usually, this is the time for me to wake up, and my clients don't call at this hour. I don't encourage clients to call me before 9 a.m. Conversations about court cases so early in the morning fill the entire day with an unbearable cacophony. I reach for the phone and pick it up from the side table.

Someone is repeating my name to make sure that he is calling the right person.

'Yes, it's me.' I pick up the packet of cigarettes from the side table and pull one out of it.

'I am sorry to call so early in the morning.' This is the officer in charge of the mofussil police station.

'Anything important?' I know him. We frequently come across one another in the course of court cases. As a defence lawyer, I maintain a good rapport with them.

'Do you know a woman named Aisha?'

'Yes, she is my client, if that's the Aisha you are talking about.' I stop midway to light my cigarette, which I hold between my lips.

'Yes, that's the Aisha I am talking about, sir. You both were together last night?'

I keep the lighter on the table. The cigarette is hanging from my lower lip, unlit. 'Sir? Is there anything wrong?' After all, why would a policeman take an interest in a lawyer's personal life?

'She was murdered last night. She was burned to death.'

Have I woken up from my dream, or is this a morbid extension of it? Cold sweat flows from my pores. Before I can think of anything else, I find that the receiver has slipped from my hands. It lies still in my lap. My eyes see Aisha waving her torch, standing tall like a lighthouse. And now, Aisha has been murdered. She has been burned alive!

The day is bright outside, but my room has suddenly become dark as if I were in a cold mortuary whose air conditioners have been suddenly switched off. I feel the receiver in my lap, wherein a voice crackles spasmodically. I feel as if the receiver and microphone are two eyes staring at me in astonishment. I pick up the handset.

'Sir?' The sub-inspector is repeating his words over and over again. 'Is everything all right? I am afraid I heard some bizarre sound.'

I fail to find proper words. I should say something.

'Sir, can you hear me?'

'Yes, I can hear you.' I take the receiver in my other hand and stub out the unlit cigarette in the ashtray. 'The... the phone slipped out of my hand. I think you were saying something about Aisha?'

'So, you had the information about her murder!' I hear the sub-inspector's voice from the other side.

'No,' I say. 'I am hearing about this for the first time. Forgive me, I am a little upset by this news. She was my client, but there was something more between Aisha and me. We were going to get married soon.'

'I can imagine. I hope you are sitting down right now. If you are standing, please take a seat. According to her maid, the murder was committed by her elder son. Yesterday, the mother and son had a long fight over something that went on till late into the night, when the son had hit his mother with a heavy object. The maid could only see this much from the window, and then she locked herself in a room with the two children. The son is missing, but we found the mother's charred body on the floor. Maybe the boy poured kerosene on her and tried to set her on fire to make sure that she was dead.'

The voice floats in through the receiver continuously, and though I have my ear to the earpiece, I can hardly make out anything. At last, when I realize it, I try to listen attentively, but there is silence on the other side. I put down the receiver and rest my head on the wall. My head is heavy like a stone, as if the whole room is pressing me down.

Chapter Five

SITTING IN MY CHAIR, I AM STARING AT THE WALL when Mir enters with a tray of tea. He looks at my face. Maybe he has come to know of the incident. He sets down the tray and quietly leaves the room. He closes the door behind him. The storm that was raging yesterday outside the house is now raging inside me, even as there is absolute silence in the house. The tick-tock of the clock continues. Tears flow down my cheeks without my knowing it and have started to dry up, although I don't know why I am crying. I feel very bad about Aisha, but somehow, the death has fallen short of sinking into my soul. Then what name should I give to my yearning for Aisha until this morning? I take out my handkerchief and wipe my face. I place both my hands in my lap and stay for a long time in the same position. I don't know why this is so, but once again, I feel very sleepy. I rest my head on the side wall and fall into a deep slumber.

Around afternoon, an inspector comes from the police station. He narrates the incident in detail. Initially, the maid had locked herself in a room with the children, but when she smelled smoke, she panicked, and leaving the children in the room, came out screaming loudly. By that time, some people from the bakery and neighbourhood had assembled at the gate. Nadir had already disappeared with his father's gun. When people entered the room, they found the door ajar. The fire had died down inside the room. The floor was wet, and the half-burnt body of Aisha was lying on the floor in a pool of water. The inspector has brought two constables with him for my protection. He is sure that Nadir will try to kill me. I have already been attacked before. They are afraid that this matter may take a political turn. Long after he is gone, I continue to sit alone in the room, staring blankly at the wall. Then I call Kaku. The phone rings and rings, but no one answers the call. By that time, my nerves are in my control. I ask Mir to take care of the constables, to see to their food and lodging. Mir isn't worried at all. Life in prison has taught him how to face a situation like this. He has already locked the front gate, as also the back door. But there is an alcove under the staircase leading to a room whose wooden door opens out into the backstreet. I have only entered that room once or twice in my entire life. It is always empty and full of dirt. It has no windows. I have never understood the purpose of this room. Perhaps it is a relic of feudal times, a sort of dungeon that played a dubious role in the past. I send Mir to enquire about Kaku's health. He is worried about my safety. He is reluctant to leave me alone. I force him to go. Kaku's house is locked from the outside. On making enquiries with the locals, he comes to know that Kaku's son had tried to commit suicide again. But the matter was more serious in nature this time. Mir visits the hospital. Kaku's son is struggling between life and death, but there is more probability that he will pull through. I am supposed to be in the hospital at such a crucial time.

Both the constables have settled down on the veranda. A bed has been arranged for them in a small room. They never forget to stand up and salute me every time I come out. I leave the room rarely to avoid this. In the evening, I call the police station. Aisha's postmortem report has come. It says that she died last night around 10 o'clock. She was hit on the head with a heavy object, but the cause of her death was burning. She must have been unconscious when the kerosene was poured over her. A police checkpoint has been set up near Aisha's house. Although the locale of the crime falls within the jurisdiction of the suburban police, all the stations, including the town police, have been alerted with a lookout. A posse of policemen has been deputed to hunt down Nadir. They are sure he must be somewhere in the city, biding his time to attack me. I don't know why this is, but I feel no emotion. Is this the outcome of handling murder cases for so many years that I have been transformed into a statue carved of stone, without any heart to beat or eyes with light therein?

The weather doesn't change until evening. It then rains all the way into the night. I can't remember if I have ever seen such bad weather in our city. I take out my grandfather's rifle; the licence has been passed on to my name. Mir and I clean it.

He has done this many times before, and although this gun remains in my custody, I sometimes leave it with him. As he hands me the clean rifle, his eyes unconsciously fall on the framed photograph of my father. I have never told him about my father's suicide bid, but like all things in this house, he must have come to know of it. Perhaps the walls of our house leak out all its secrets. Mir is waiting to take back the rifle.

'Don't worry, it's not the same gun as you think.' I look carefully at the gun and fake a smile to reassure him. But my smile is so hollow that he sees through it. He also smiles in response, but can it really be called a smile? My gun is a costly double-barrelled weapon, a .375 H&H Magnum which uses 9.5 mm bullets. As I peer into the barrel of my gun, I once again look back at my father's photo. His eyes have a strange glint, as if they have acquired a new life of their own, or maybe I am imagining things. The gun that he used to commit suicide is now in the police strongroom. I never tried to get it back. That involves a long legal hassle. Mir does not budge an inch until I give back the gun. He doesn't hide his distrust of me with it. His attitude tells me that if it comes to it, he will not hesitate to snatch it out of my hand. But he doesn't know that in addition to this gun, I also have an automatic pistol, whose licence I had acquired on the grounds of self-defence as a criminal lawyer, though my close relationship with a district magistrate was more helpful in acquiring it. I don't stop Mir from taking the gun. When I come out into the veranda, I see that a constable is teaching Mir how to pull the trigger. He is using his own cartridges for this purpose, which aren't made for a Magnum. I haven't handed over the Magnum bullets to Mir.

'It's a beautiful gun,' the constable declares. 'Its price will not be less than two hundred thousand.'

'Mir,' I say in a peremptory tone, 'put the gun back in the closet. Whatever be the circumstances, you are not going to use it.'

As I take back the gun, a strange smile flashes on his lips. I know that if the circumstances so warranted, he will not hesitate to fire it without bothering about the consequences. Who knows, he might already be in possession of some rounds of bullets, purloined in the course of cleaning the rifle all these years. I shut the door of my room, open the locker of the steel closet and take out a blue packet. Wrapped inside a heavy muslin cloth is my pistol. I feel the weight of it as I take it in my hand, which must be barely six hundred grams without the bullets. This pocket pistol is a single-action, semi-automatic German Mauser Model 1934, which I had bought from a retired colonel, who had fought valiantly at some European front during the Second World War, standing shoulder to shoulder with the British army. He must have pulled off some commendable stunt because not only was he given this pistol as a bravery prize, but a road in Kolkata was also named after him. I don't know whether that road still carries his name or whether it has vanished from the street map of the city. Towards the end of his life, the colonel became an alcoholic. I never met him, but the shopkeeper of the weapons store in Lal Bazar, from where I had bought this pistol, had all the information ready for customers. This wasn't a pistol that could hit targets very far off, but then, I didn't intend to hunt a lion or an elephant, did I? I release the safety valve and pull the slide back. The magazine pops out. Presently, all its eight chambers are empty. I pull the trigger, and slamming the slide shut, I pull it once again, and the hammer drops. Repeating this action time and again, I make sure that both of us are fully ready. I rotate the pin and remove its small-sized barrel from the frame. I check the other parts of the pistol several times. I take out a tin box from the lowermost shelf of the closet, put it on the table and open it. It contains cotton swabs, a brush, a bottle of oil, thin iron needles and cloth rags. The cloth rags are still caked with soot from the last cleaning, and there is a little bit of machine oil left in the bottle. I clean the parts using the rags and the brush, I oil them and assemble the weapon again. Once more, I place my index finger on the trigger and try to aim at an imagined target on the wall and then lower the muzzle. Despite some small hitches, it has the look of a pocket-sized pistol with an astonishing level of thumb safety. As soon as you press the safety, the slide locks on its own, which reduces the chances of the pistol firing unintentionally. On the other hand, to get it ready to be fired, you only need to press the button on the grip, and the pistol immediately becomes ready to be fired. As I caress the cool surface of the black pistol, I can't remember a time in the history of this city when people used pistols or guns. Except for the double-barrel guns that people fire in the sky at wedding ceremonies or during festivals, or those locally made guns that are fired in the air to disperse the mob by dacoits who hail from neighbouring districts, in the course of their annual foray of looting Marwari businessmen or raiding their cashboxes. I take out another plastic bag from the locker, which has tiny 7.65 mm bullets. I keep rolling a bullet between my thumb and middle finger, and as I rotate it, I ponder on the astonishing feat of mankind, who has created such a beautiful thing to write the saga of their own devastation. I put the pistol and the bullets back in the polythene bag and close the locker. Three days have passed since that incident. I have started going to court under the protection of my bodyguards, but I don't stay there very long. The rain stopped two days ago, but there are still clouds in the sky.

'They are not going anywhere without a huge storm first.' Mir stares out the window as he sets down evening tea at the table. He repeats himself.

'How can you be so sure of it?' I say. 'I see no sign of a storm on the horizon. These are monsoon clouds on the way back to the ocean. I think they have rained down all their water. There might be a drizzle or something, and that would be all.'

'No,' he says with conviction. 'I see a huge storm brewing somewhere. I am an expert in reading the sky. In my prison days, all I had was the sky.'

'That does not make you a weather expert.' I dismiss him and start drinking tea.

Mir has been looking for Jhabra everywhere. He is not anywhere in the house. I am sure that the animal has left for good. It was a local breed. Mir never put him on a leash. He had put a collar around his neck only after I warned him of the municipal people going after street dogs. The dog would be allowed off and on to leave the house and come back on his own. This had to do with the idea that he should be allowed some freedom to satisfy his sexual urges. Mir wasn't stingy when it came to feeding him. He didn't have any proper place to sleep, nor was there any place in the house reserved for him. He would always be found at the staircase of the gardener's vacant quarter, with his tongue lolling out. He had a habit of barking at clients when they left the house. But he was not allowed at the gate. I felt that Mir had a special attachment to the dog, but he was aware that it was a local breed. One day, I hear a strange sound, as if someone is scratching the wall somewhere inside the house. I am busy with some clients when Mir enters the room. His hair is dishevelled. His eyes exude a strange terror. He has also heard the sound.

'Have you searched the house completely?' I ask him after hearing from him. My clients look at us with disbelief. They don't get why we would be so worried about a local breed.

'He is not in the house.'

'You have yet to learn a lot of things about this house. I mean those rooms which remain always shut.'

After getting rid of my clients, I light a cigarette and relax in my chair when Mir rushes in gasping for breath. 'Jhabra is dying.' He has tears in his eyes. 'Someone has poisoned him.' I follow him into a small room in the basement. The door is partly open, one part of it hanging askew on its hinges. Perhaps it has not been opened for so many years and the hinges had come loose when the door was opened by force. A foul smell lurks in the room. Jhabra lies on the floor. He tries to open his eyes as the torchlight falls on him. He is covered in his own excreta and vomit.

'He has been poisoned, or maybe some snake bit him,' I say. 'Shut the door. We can't do anything before it is morning. I don't know of any veterinary doctor in this city.'

But it's futile to wait till morning. Jhabra is on the verge of death. Around midnight, Mir carries him in his arms and goes outside. I can't believe that Nadir has any knowledge about dogs, or he will go so far as to think of poisoning one. Mir doesn't come back by the time I am ready for court.

'Sir, for a few days, you should avoid coming here,' a constable says. He has come to replace a constable in the courtroom. In the absence of Kaku, I have brought Nripen with me. 'Some people in the police station suspect that the killer has been roaming around the Chinese Mansion. A senior officer has asked us to give this message to you.'

The Chinese Mansion! So, Nadir has discovered it. We are

getting closer. When I return home in the afternoon, I see some more policemen. Mir is in their custody. The policemen are in civil attire.

'Is it your servant?'

'Yes?'

'He might have taken advantage of your absence. He was roaming about with your gun. We were keeping an eye on him. Today, we finally caught him at a nearby drain. When we interrogated him, we found that he didn't have a licence. On top of that, he is a prisoner who has served his sentence and works at your home.' A man steps forward and places the gun on the table. I pick it up and look at it. It's indeed my gun, and it's empty. Seeing me open the chamber of the rifle, a policeman places the cartridges taken out of it along with a few extra ones on the table. I look at Mir with astonishment. My fear was not unfounded. He must have been stashing those away while cleaning the gun. He stands like a criminal with his head down. 'We discussed with our senior officer. He knows about this gun. We haven't registered any case against him, but we want you to keep an eye on him. He is loyal to you. Ever since he served his sentence years ago, there hasn't been any news of his involvement in any criminal activity, but if he uses this gun, you will be in a huge mess. You must already know this as a lawyer.'

'Do you want to go to prison again?' I look at Mir after the police are gone. 'Put the gun back. Don't even touch it without my permission.'

'We are not safe in the house. He must be around somewhere,' Mir says. 'Every time I stand on the roof, I feel like I am seeing his shadow somewhere. Do you think that the police are doing their job sincerely? It will be too late by the time they catch him. I have never seen a single policeman doing his duty behind the Chinese Mansion.'

'That's because they are in civil attire. And keep your prejudices to yourself. Rather, leave the gun here. I don't trust you.'

'I don't want this gun.' He places the gun on the table. 'I can strangle him with my bare hands.'

'You won't ever do anything. This isn't your fight. It looks like you haven't learnt anything from your experience in jail. And what have you done with Jhabra?'

'Jhabra is alive. The doctor's medicine is working. These stray dogs are very gritty. The doctor said that the diarrhoea and vomiting saved him from certain death. Maybe he ate something he shouldn't have.'

I stare at him in disbelief. I am not convinced that he won't do anything rash tomorrow or the day after tomorrow. Perhaps it's the outcome of what he had said that I go to the terrace and look around. An eerie silence prevails in the neighbourhood. Most of the roofs and terraces are blackened with soot, except for one roof where a middle-aged woman, with hair as white as hemp, is spreading clothes on a line. All the roofs are vacant and quiet; in fact, there isn't even a single pigeon on any of the TV antennas. Only in some places, clothes are swaying in the wind. The windows of the Chinese Mansion are shut. The small door built into its large gate is open. Missing the sun, the day looks dull. The road itself and all the trees along it stand still and lifeless. I listen attentively.

I can hear the sound of water from the river. Or it might be my imagination. Maybe the servant is right. If you stand here and look around, you can't help the feeling that someone is watching you. Nadir! Anger boils up inside me like lava. The dead sub-inspector was right; maybe we have entered a very delicate era when children don't shy away from making the most fatal decisions. If you see it from this point of view, there is so much similarity between the death of Aisha and that of Payal! The only difference is that Payal was an animal, and killing her was an easy sport, whereas Aisha as a human being was not, and now, Nadir is at the mercy of the law. After returning to my room, I take out my pistol. I open its safety valve, push back its slide and fill the magazine chamber with bullets. I push in the chamber and hold the pistol like I am shooting it. Once again, it is pointed at the wall. I have a strange feeling as I look at it. The pistol is completely ready, an angel of death who can never be punished. I put the muzzle between my jaws. It is cold and smells of oil. It's simply a matter of pulling the trigger; my brain will explode out of my head, and the whole episode will be over. I will be out of the dark tunnel. I remember my father. If only he had used a pistol that day, he wouldn't have had to endure such agony for eight years. No weapon is as successful as a pistol when it comes to suicide. All you need to do is place it in the proper spot. And as I am busy with the pistol like this, I think, *Maybe this time, the city will hear a real bullet being fired.* I take out the muzzle from my mouth and wipe it with the help of a towel.

The next day, putting the pistol in my pants pocket, I enter the dank basement through the alcove. Mir must have been using this basement room to go out of the house when the constables were on duty. And all along, I had been under the illusion that he didn't know anything about this house. The room's inner door opens under a termite-laden wooden staircase, most of its steps broken. As it was not dependable, after my father's demise, I had to build a concrete staircase that led straight to the corridor. I open the door. I see fingerprints on its muddy surface. The other door opening outside into the lane has similar patterns. These must be Mir's footprints. I shut the door behind me and start for the street. I don't look back. I know that Mir will be somewhere, keeping an eye on me. This path is not a thoroughfare – a mere gaping hole between the boundary walls of the houses that stand on both sides. There is a concrete drain running along the wall, overgrown with bushes. I hardly cross a few houses when, with the undergrowth and thorny bushes on the way, it becomes difficult for me to walk; in fact, it becomes impossible to set foot anywhere. I jump over the remains of what had once been a boundary wall. This is an empty three-storey building.

Passing under its fire escape, whose iron railings and broken steps are hanging precariously on the wall, I emerge on the road. Across it is a low plain with a lone house in the middle, thatched with country tiles. In the past, it used to be a place where human corpses would be dissected, but now, that house is not a part of the hospital. My house and the Chinese Mansion are a good distance from this place. There is no sun in the sky. No wonder the trees look dull and colourless. Not a single bird anywhere, as if the storm that had been raging two days ago had carried them away. There is a slow wind. To protect myself from the cold, I wind my muffler around my ears and take a walk to the forest behind the Chinese Mansion. Soon, under a blue sky, its upper floors become visible, offering a glimpse of its windows among the trees. I don't know why, but I feel as if Nadir is present somewhere close by. It does not matter to me. When you have a pistol in your hand, all your fears dissipate. You feel so self-confident and safe. After all, Nadir is a child; if he and I have a face-off, I will easily overpower him. I have no idea whether he knows how to cock a gun, and if he is capable of it, may god bless him with 100 per cent success. This will be better for both of us. I don't want to die like my father, suffering a long spell of agony. However, if he misses his target, or shows a lack of skill, this pistol will be handy for me to finish the job. I am sure that in such a situation I won't hesitate to empty all the bullets into him, or if it goes from bad to worse, on myself. And as I am satisfied that in either case I am not going to lose anything, suddenly I feel that I am taking the matter too far. He is not a professional killer. There is a probability that he will lose his nerves when we stand face to face holding our guns in hand. And even if he doesn't back out, I am capable enough of injuring him. In case he gets killed, it is not going to be the worst-case scenario for him because he will be saved from the long arm of the law and sure imprisonment with hard labour that is waiting for him. He is no more a minor. There is a probability that he might be hanged for double murder. As I walk between the trees, I suddenly feel sorry for him. A man's life is not solely his own. It connects him with a lot of people. This is the biggest irony – that a man does not die alone. Worn out from hunger and thirst, that young boy must be missing his two brothers, or maybe the urge for revenge has completely numbed his mind. It's not possible for him to roam about with a rifle in broad daylight. Nowadays, long-range rifles aren't very useful. You can't move freely with them. You may be nabbed like Mir. Such people also become the butt of jokes in society. Even with your licence, you might end up in a police station. Whatever may be the case, he must be lurking somewhere in the bush like a hungry wolf, sure of his prey moving unaware of its fate, but he cannot be so certain of it. Am I providing him a target out of sympathy? What else can be the reason for my coming out in the open, giving a slip to my guards? If I shoot him, it will be the first time in my life that I am shooting any man. It's better if no shoot-out takes place, or let it be the last bullet of my life, completely successful in its purpose, unlike my father's, whose soul couldn't fly out of the hole of his head, because of which he had to live a long life as a vegetable. I can still see the blood dripping from that hole.

After walking a few yards in the opposite direction, I stop at an incline. A clump of trees stands there at the drain that originates behind the Chinese Mansion. This place isn't as grubby as it used to be before. Perhaps some sort of cleaning work has taken place recently. People come from far-off places to the Chinese Mansion. They sometimes need this place for some odd purpose. Despite standing there for a long time, I don't see anyone behind the tree trunks, nor do I hear footsteps crackle on dried leaves. Fed up with the silence, I set out for the river. Maybe I won't be able to spot him. In that case, it will be better that he finds me.

The river water is overflowing its bank. Boats are plying in it; one of them has even hoisted a sail that is swelling like the belly of a pregnant woman. It's hard to believe that at other times people would cross this river on foot or in rickshaws. I am on the steps of the cremation ground, sitting alone. This is the last refuge for mankind, the very kingdom of death. Maybe we will come face to face in this place. No, I reassure myself, this is not the place for death. When the whole process of death is over, when no more of life is left in the drama of living, when death itself is dead and when time leaves a cold stinking body in its wake, it is then time for this place. From this point of view, this place has nothing to do with death. The last steps of the ghat are inundated in water forming small whirlpools at various places. Branches, leaves and bushes are adrift in the water; even tussocks with mud sticking to grass are swirling. A bamboo mat quickly passes by, carried along by the water, one edge of it singed. Perhaps upstream, the water has been let out from the dam. This is the misfortune of this river. When its bed is dry, the dam closes its water gates tight, and when it is next to impossible for the river to manage the flow of water, the dam floods it. As the Bengalis say: *It's like pouring more oil on a human head that is already overflowing with oil.* I go up, sit on a damp wall and look at the sky. Dull clouds hang there. They give the impression of someone having strewn ash in the sky. Taking my hand to my back, I grope for the gun that I have stuffed between my backbone and belt. A human being is such a strange creature. Willing or not, once in a while, he is forced to take some decision, however ridiculous that might be, because if he doesn't do that, what's the point of coming into this world? On the other hand, if he does it, he becomes a mere pawn in a game of chess that moves in accordance with someone else's game plan. No wonder, when there are consequences, he does believe in them. So, what does he think? He thinks that this can't be the outcome of my will. I am sitting in absolute silence at this point and waiting eagerly for an attack so that I can return it with all my vehemence. What a wonder it is that I am not at all afraid for my life. Maybe I had never loved my life; I was simply living it or, as people say,

I had been just whiling away my time, dragging it along from morning till evening. Apparently, I had been making all sorts of worldly decisions, but inside me was a numb human being who had nothing to do with those decisions, as if my own life had been a protracted court case which, as a professional, I had to carry on coldly to its logical conclusion. In another sense, I had failed to understand what this life is. It might be that living my life without any purpose had unknowingly pushed me towards Aisha, disregarding the fact that Nadir was rapidly growing up into a man and could raise a storm. As the elderly sub-inspector had rightly put down in his letter, there was nothing unnatural about this attack; in fact, as an experienced lawyer, I should have foreseen it as an absolute certainty. Maybe I was aware that Nadir was growing up, but the numb man inside me, under the pressure of animal urges, needed some sort of provocation for its blood to boil up. Perhaps I wasn't any different from my father. I am sure that the dire circumstances were his own making, which had ultimately led him to take up the gun and aim it at his own face. But why do I feel that if Nadir materializes from thin air, not only will I fail to defend myself, but I also won't even be able to aim my pistol at him? I am buried in these thoughts when I hear footsteps. I turn around. No one is there, either on the steps of the cremation grounds or up on the road. There is only the tremor of leaves in the wind or invisible insects wriggling in the bushes that I can feel in my bones. On a day when there is neither sun in the sky nor darkness on the earth, I have come out to the riverbank as if in search of death itself, and as I walk in this desolate place, gazing at the river water that flows with an immense force, I look at the sky, where sparks are flying in the ashes, as if I am in the grip of a hope that this is going to be the last evening of my life. There was a time when this river was a symbol of hope for me; today, I have come here in search of death. In a way, this river and its bank are not real by any stretch of the imagination; they are there because I have conjured them up. Aisha herself, Nadir and her children were nothing but characters in a drama, whose script has been written by me. Is it not the onus now on my shoulder to carry it to its climax? Tomorrow, all this river water may flow down the river to vanish into the sea, leaving in its wake the same old desert. The bank across the river will still be waiting for me till the end of my life.

I leave the cremation grounds behind. People are moving on the river slope. A child is running his tricycle hard by the water. His mother drags him back to a safer place. Every time she does this, she chuckles and looks back at me in utter helplessness. My gaze falls on a crow that is dragging a dead kitten to a bush. The entrails of the kitten are hanging out, completely shrivelled up. I think how similar both the hunter and the prey are. I hear the voices of people. These are the same gamblers who I always see in this spot. Behind them are the same endless rows of houses with roofs of country tiles. A mighty gust of wind is scattering the smoke over the tiles. The sky has become black, its edges set ablaze by the sun.

'Hey, Rangi!' One of the gamblers calls out to the woman who is gathering dry leaves in her bamboo basket. 'Want to go behind the bush?'

The girl is scared. She becomes stiff. She is a pitiful sight, forced to be an adult long before her time. She is already an old woman, though she must be in the prime of her youth.

'She has had abortions countless times.' A gambler looks at me and winks. 'Look, look, she is acting coy as if she is a virgin. This basket is just for show. Her real business starts after sundown.'

My fingers take the pistol in their grip. I try to avoid the eyes of the gamblers. An armed man is a dangerous thing; he can do anything in the spur of the moment. The girl is probably lame in one leg. She walks with a limp. I don't know why my standing there with my hand in my pocket gives her the impression that I might give her some money. She stops her work and, smiling coyly, extends her emaciated palm before me.

'Please give me a rupee, babu!'

My hand involuntarily comes out of my pocket. I don't have my wallet with me. When a man takes up a mission of death, a wallet is the last thing on his mind.

The gamblers laugh out loud when they find that my hand has come out empty. The woman has all the hatred of the world in her eyes. It's impossible to convince her that I don't have any money, that while I had put my hand inside my pocket, all I wanted was to grip my pistol. She must be under the impression that I pulled a cruel joke on her. I hear her hurling abuse at me. The laughter of the gamblers follows my footsteps.

The constables don't believe their eyes when they see me turn up at the gate. Mir rushes from the veranda and unlocks the door. It's clear from the way he looks at me that he is not one bit surprised that he is seeing me enter the house now, without him ever seeing me leave. He might have followed me and come back home before my return. He looks relaxed. The belongings of both the constables are packed and ready. They are waiting in the veranda for transportation. They have been recalled to their duty at the police station. The police found Nadir. He had hung himself from a tree not too far from the Chinese Mansion. He had stolen a dhoti from a clothesline when the washerman wasn't there. The gun was discovered among the reeds by the side of the river. When he had escaped with the gun, he had no idea that it was useless without cartridges, or perhaps he had dropped the box of cartridges somewhere. His body was hidden behind leafy branches. People had come to know of its existence because a swarm of kites and crows had gathered over the tree. The street dogs had also gathered at the roots, and raising their heads upwards, they were barking at the top of their voices. Nadir had deep gashes in his head; maybe birds of prey or rodents had brutally attacked him. The blood had flown down his face and congealed on his body. He had been spotted in the morning, although there was every probability that he might have committed suicide two days ago. He was identified by the people from his grandfather's house, as also by the maid. His body had been sent off to the mortuary. I can imagine his body undergoing autopsy. Once the autopsy is done, the body will be sewn up and handed over to his maternal grandfather. He will be buried in their private graveyard, by the side of his grandfather's grave. I don't know where they might have buried Aisha. At night, I get a call from the police station. The post-mortem report is in. Nadir's fingers had burn marks on them. He had probably tried to stop the fire after pouring oil on his mother. Perhaps the countdown to his own death had begun at that point.

I stay awake till late into the night. Today, I have taken more than my usual intake of drinks. Mir has made many unsuccessful attempts to take away the bottle and glass. The gusts of wind that had taken the form of a storm are slowing down. Through a window of my chamber, I can see the upper floor of my own house. It vanishes in the rain and then comes into view. Mir stands with his back to the window. Maybe Nadir's death has left a bad scar on his psyche.

Yes, faces... all that matters are faces. They don't let us live. They never die; they are always there, waiting for us in one form or another. This won't be an ordinary night for me; on the other hand, Mir will be forced to live his normal life from tomorrow morning. What else can we human beings do?

I look out of the window where the storm is raging again. Maybe Mir was right – this gale won't stop without a big storm making short shrift of everything. I have dragged the chair to the window, and sitting alone, I feel like someone has been disgorging my intestines, heart, kidneys and all, turning me into an empty shell, devoid of any emotion, a sort of skeleton covered with skin, with eyes burning in their sockets. The wind is whistling through the chinks of the window. There is no life in my eyes. Someone is calling me. I look at the sky, which is dark. No, this can't go on like this. I open the closet and then the locker, and once again, stuff the pistol in my belt against my spine. The dark dungeon... I have now begun to understand its purpose. I look at the sky again. Wait for me!

The dungeon is dark. Closing the outer door behind me, I emerge at the drain, where shockingly, it's daytime. The sky is clear, as if I have entered a different world. I turn my head and take a look at our house. My god, what I see is beyond my comprehension! The sky is a canvas divided into two different parts; one has night in it with clouds and dark houses, whereas it is broad daylight in the other half, and dividing these two parts, there is a zigzag line, as if lightning has torn the world asunder. Shaking off this strange vision from my eyes, I walk alongside the drain and reach the three-storey house. I jump over the remnants of the boundary wall and, walking under the fire escapes, emerge on the road where the defunct mortuary stands. I am within sight of the Chinese Mansion. No power in the world can stop me from entering it today. The mansion is completely silent. It looks so high from its boundary wall. I knock at the wooden gate.

It doesn't open. I don't have time to wait. No face appears in any of the windows despite my endless knocking at the door. Neither can I hear the sound of footsteps inside. There is no human voice anywhere. I push the small door. It opens inside with a groan. I put my left foot in and bend my head to enter.

As I straighten up, there is no Chinese Mansion anywhere. I am alone in the middle of an undulating plain that rolls onto the horizon with the sun shining like a blazing orange. A few kilometres away in the north, there is the silhouette of a village surrounded by palm trees. It is so vivid, as if the intervening distance means nothing to it. A strong wind is blowing in the fields. It becomes faster by the time I reach the village. It is icy cold, but I don't have any warm clothes to save myself from the wind. Though both my feet are bare, I don't have any trouble walking on the soil. Pebbles and stones cover the earth, but they don't prick my soles. I am taking long strides without giving any thought to the pistol that has started knocking on my spine. I reach outside the village, where, in a field, the old man waits for me with his umbrella. He stands up and says, 'Namaskar.' He leads me to the village across the field. There are fiery red flowers in the *palash* trees.

The tin roofs of houses shimmer in the sun. On the parapet of the well, there is a wooden shaft; the two wooden beams jut out like human arms holding nothing. The water wheels are gone. The black-faced monkey sits atop the wall of the government primary school. This time, it is not interested in us. The woman is waiting for us in her courtyard. A long veil is drawn over her face. Goats are resting in the shadow of a house, chewing cud.

'Take me to the crime scene,' I tell the old man. It is so lonely here.

'Huzoor, you have covered such a long distance barefoot. At least have a glass of water.'

'No, I am not thirsty. And if I delay it, there won't be anything left for me to do.'

'Anyway, you are already late, huzoor,' the old man says. 'People are always late. Or people do it on purpose.'

The woman sobs into her veil.

'You are saying something that I have heard a hundred times before,' I say. 'Maybe I don't need you to guide me. I know my way.'

'I can give you company at least till the drain.'

We cross a market and come out in an open field, leaving the village behind. We reach the arid drain. There, between huge boulders, stand some palm trees. The path twists and turns a lot before it reaches the jujube orchard. The old man falls behind. I see him last near a boulder. He is staring into the void like a blind man. The gate is made of thorny branches. It is flung open as if someone is expecting me. I take out the pistol and walk among the trees.

This is the season of jujube. The trees are laden with green, yellow and red berries. In a corner, where the wall built over a rock is quite high, the rapist stands all by himself, staring at the girl, who is lying spreadeagled on the dirt. Her frock has been pulled up to her chest. Black blood is oozing through her bare legs. Both her eyes are open. Flies are buzzing on her eyeballs. He turns his head and casts a glance at me. His long, wavy hair is trembling in the wind, his fat nostrils are flared up. There is a strange smile on his face. He doesn't say anything. The pistol in my hand does not have any effect on him. Does he know the havoc it can wreak on him?

'You can't turn your silence into a weapon.' I speak to him as I move the pistol. 'You had not uttered a single word during the case.'

He doesn't react to my question. His smile is plastered on his face.

'Is she dead?' I ask. He shakes his head in the negative. 'You are lying. She is already dead inside. She cannot come to life again. She has been forced to live all her life like a corpse. I have seen the doctor's report. Her uterus is a total mess. She has lost her capacity to bear a child. Why don't you put your hands behind your neck and kneel? It will be easier for you to die that way.'

He follows my command and gets down on his knees. He interlocks his fingers behind his neck. His ugly face is held upwards. I go behind him and put the muzzle on the back of his head. I feel the toughness of his skull bone. The skin sinks under the pressure from the muzzle. He is staring blankly at the top of the wall. A white cloud hangs motionless in the sky. I look at the child's body, spreadeagled on the earth, flies buzzing on her private parts.

'You like young girls, right? And she isn't the first girl in your life, am I right?' He doesn't reply.

'Aren't you scared of death?'

He doesn't answer. I flare up in anger.

'You can't use your silence on me.' I pull the safety lock and place my finger on the trigger. His body doesn't move. It doesn't even twitch as I pull the trigger. The bullet enters his skull with an explosion. He is still on his knees with his fingers behind his neck, as if the bullet had no effect on him. Then his body jerks, and he falls to the ground. The bullet has pierced through his forehead. His head is on the earth, blood curdling around it like a mushroom. He is not dead. There is still life in his legs. He is trying to stand up like a blind man, placing his hand on the earth. Under the impact of my second bullet, he collapses on the ground. I put on the safety lock and stuff the pistol in its place. Once again, I cast a look at the girl's lifeless body; the sky has suddenly become dark. Lightning flashes on the horizon. Despite the mist, I can see the Chinese Mansion. It is just a few furlongs away. There is light in its windows. I turn around and take long strides towards it. By the time I reach it, the world has become pitch-black. There is a big crowd in its backyard. My jaw drops as I reach near it. Hundreds of cats are moving atop the walls, doors and windows of the Chinese Mansion. Roaring and screeching wildly, they are pouring forth in hordes. Provoked by my presence, they are racing towards me. They may surround me any time now. I run towards the gate, but its small door is shut tight. Someone has locked it from outside. I can feel the screeching and roaring cats behind me. Some cats lunge at me, and soon, they are on my body, tugging at my pants, climbing on my shoulders. I try to find my pistol, but I have dropped it somewhere. The cats are increasing in number; their sharp claws are ripping my clothes apart, tearing down my face. It's impossible for me to stand up on my feet. Weighed down by cats, I fall on my back, and like a blind man, try to shake them off. The cats have also come crumbling down to the earth with me. Suddenly, there is a loud explosion, and they all freeze. The gate is flung open; my father stands holding his rifle. He aims it at the Chinese Mansion and fires. The cats flee through the spiral staircase, squealing and howling. They are all disappearing into the caverns of the building. Father is loading his gun and firing volley after volley, until the entire Chinese Mansion becomes empty and quiet. There is not a single cat anywhere. I lie prone on the ground, covered in my own blood. Father bends over me and picks me up on his shoulder; my eyes are shut. Holding his gun in one hand and me on his shoulder, he is walking. My blood is entering my eyes, through which I can see a spiral staircase vanish into the darkness. A door opens somewhere. Father is laying me down on my bed.

I hear his voice. 'Now you may open your eyes.' I open my eyes. He is standing beside the bed, bending over me with a look of affection in his eyes. His bald head is drenched in sweat, the hair on his earlobes is frazzled, his shirt buttons are undone and his eyes are bloodshot. He hugs me, and after planting a kiss on my forehead runs his trembling fingers through my hair. His breath reeks of alcohol. 'Why don't you take a nap?' He says it over and over again. 'The Chinese Mansion will never bother you again.' I shut my eyes, if not for anything, just to get rid of him. Who knows what time it is. I open my eyes and look around. I am alone in my bed, resting my elbows on the pillow. I look at the sky, where there are long streaks of lightning. Big drops of rain hit the windowpanes with a thud, creating a strange sound. I feel drowsy. It's difficult for me to know if I am awake or asleep. A strong wind is bringing rain across the road through a blanket of mist as another strong cross-current of wind brings cold water into my room. One of the windows flies open. I get off my bed and take a few steps to try to latch it up when my gaze falls on the Chinese Mansion. Its huge golden gate is wide open. A chocolate-coloured coffin is coming out.

The Chinese lantern is hanging from its electric wire. Pressed on by the wind, it sways to one side like a balloon. My eyes widen in wonder. Innumerable torches are throwing human shadows in the empty spaces between the pillars. Their beams are fusing together, forming dark and dim shadows, shadows intermingling or cutting across each other, getting stuck and then splitting up again. Some of these shadows hold umbrellas. They are opening and closing vehicle doors.

I hear footsteps at the door. It's Mir holding an emergency light. Shadows come alive in the room, totally different from the ones the tubelight or table lamp usually create in the room. He hands me a towel, and opening the wardrobe, brings out a nightdress that he spreads on the bed.

'I came to your room twice. You were seeing some nightmare, I think.'

'Look at the gate of the Chinese Mansion. They are taking out a coffin,' I say as I dry my head with the towel.

Mir goes to the window and opens it. He throws a casual glance outside and comes back. 'The Chinese are taking their dead to the burial ground,' he says. 'There is nothing to be surprised about. This is the custom of the world. When a person dies, people come to bury him. You are worried for no reason. People will die under one pretext or another. Have I ever told you that when I was in prison, my father committed suicide? People say that the spirit of my child used to stalk him day and night.'

I look into his eyes with utter surprise. 'This coffin that you see is from fifteen years ago,' I say. 'How can you see it?'

'I know. You aren't seeing it for the first time. Nor is it the last time that you will see it.' Mir is in front of the window again, looking at the sky. 'Had I not forewarned?' He turns around and says, 'The rain will stop after a big storm.'

Light is coming through the rectangular window of the bathroom. I have just finished showering. I stand naked in front of the mirror and shave myself. I have never liked my face. Perhaps this is a phenomenon common to every human being. No one likes his face. So, what does he do? He starts searching for another face in his own, a face to his liking, and a day comes when one such face suddenly pops out from the mist. This is the start of narcissism that helps him to live his life as a new human being, enamoured of his new beauty, assuring him that he has the most beautiful face in the world, as some intellectual has said that everyone is beautiful provided you look at him or her from a particular angle. It's not like I hadn't taken my face seriously. But something weird happened to me soon after I had hit puberty. I had noticed that my face bore no resemblance to my father or grandfather. Since then, I have looked at my face umpteen times from different angles, but I never find any imprint of them in it. This has always made me nervous. This is the reason that I rarely stop before my face, letting it slip out of my field of vision.

I have finished shaving. I wash my face thoroughly and then dry it with a towel. Taking cologne into the pores of my fingers, I dab both my cheeks to rouse myself completely from sleep. I don't know why I have a feeling these days that the gap between my wakefulness and sleep is gradually vanishing. I wrap the towel around my waist and come out.

It is a sunny day on the lawn. After a long spell of rain, the day looks clean. The leaves are shining in the trees. Birds are hopping on the branches. I see a squirrel's tail sneak into the leaves. God knows in such foul weather in what place she takes refuge. I put on my clothes and enter my chamber, where Kaku is waiting in a chair reserved for visitors. Holding his head between his palms, he is mumbling something. The hair on his earlobes has turned white, his sunken eyes scream of a hangover. It is an outcome of innumerable nights passed in vigil.

'Kaku...' I place my hand on his shoulder. 'Are you all right?'

He wakes up from his reverie and looks at me. His skeletal shoulder shudders under my fingers. He is trying to gain control over his emotions but fails. He hugs me and lets out a howl. This is the first time in thirty years that I am seeing him weep so profusely. Ah, we human beings carry such tornados locked up within us. We never know that a dam exists inside us that is going to burst one day.

'He tried to commit suicide again.' His words are choked with convulsions, as if I am hearing a woman's voice. 'This time, he is badly wounded. He is in a lot of pain, but he will pull through. I told the doctors that to keep him alive is worse than his death. They think I have gone mad. How should I explain it to them? Why don't you do something for me?'

'He will be okay,' I say, placing my hand on his head.

'That's what I'm scared of,' he says.

'You shouldn't have come.'

'Are you firing me?'

'Why are you saying that?' Perhaps he had heard the news that I was going to court with Nripen.

'You can tell me frankly if you think I am no longer of any use to you. I will go my way. This old bull will find some other work for himself. He has a lot of energy left in him.'

'You aren't well. You have been through such a harrowing time.' I pat his back. 'Let's talk about it some other time.'

I am cutting open the envelopes that the postman had brought with scissors when Mir enters with my breakfast. He is avoiding eye contact with me. He is unusually quiet. Had he really come to my room last night, or was that all part of my dream? He covers the teapot with a cosy. He doesn't notice that, unlike other days, the room is dark today.

'Pull the curtains aside. It is so dark here.'

He starts to draw the curtains aside. My eyes follow him. His back is bent so low, as if the burden of life has become too cumbersome for him.

Kaku enters my chamber at 1 p.m. He has become normal. The backlog of work has changed him.

'Some clients want to meet you,' he says. 'It's a big land dispute.'

'Please send them in.'

Kaku doesn't move.

'Anything else?' I lift my head and look at him. 'He is leaving.'

'Who?' I hear footsteps at the door. Mir parts the curtain. He is with a suitcase. As our eyes meet, he enters and puts the suitcase down on the floor.

I look straight into Mir's eyes. I see that they have lost their focus.

'Congratulations, at last you have found your world.' I fidget in my chair, and resting my body on its back, stretch out my arms. Holding the hand rests with my fingers as if I am playing the piano, I look at him. He is avoiding eye contact.

'No, there is no such world in this universe,' his voice comes. For the first time, he looks straight into my eyes. This time, he is a completely different man. His gaze has that special solar ray that penetrates our eyes, and passing through the back of our head, goes on in its eternal journey.

'If you want to say something, this is the time. You see, the storm has passed.'

'All these years, you never asked me what was the thing that motivated me to come to your house after I served my sentence.'

'Because you were a man of few words. And such people never open their hearts until they themselves decide.'

'For years, I have been waiting that a day will come when you ask me this question. And then I thought, maybe you too aren't a man of this planet. When you took over my case, I was surprised. What kind of a man was this who had no qualms about defending a man who had brutally killed his wife and child? How could he take up a fight on behalf of a man who was a criminal both in the eyes of the law and god?'

'Because I am a professional. And if we start looking at cases from that angle, there won't be any cases left to fight. To be honest, I had fought your case for the sake of money.'

'No. You did not take any money to defend me. You were never paid the full amount. I had reminded my friends. They understood it at a very late stage. By then, the case was in the high court. Whatever it was that you did for me, they had a high regard for that.'

'I had started my practice as a newcomer. To come to the limelight, I needed a big case. Every new lawyer is required to pass through such ordeals. In a way, I used you.'

'No, this wasn't the reason either.' Mir shakes his head in the negative. 'I would not have found it out had I not had the opportunity to live in this house.'

'And what did you find?'

'I can't say. It's hard to express it in words. All I know is, every day in the jail, it was you who were on my mind. I would never have forgiven you for saving me from the rope.'

'It wasn't a case of hanging. Your mental condition wasn't normal when you committed the deed. As a defence lawyer, I should have understood that this could have swayed the case in your favour. In fact, let me confess it was my stupidity that ruined your case.'

'I don't know these legal twists and turns. But I hadn't come that day with any good intentions. If you had searched my body, you would have found this weapon.' He steps forward and places a knife on the table. Kaku's eyes widen in disbelief.

'I had a hunch that day that you had not come with any good intentions.' I pick up the folded knife and flick it open. I feel its sharp edge with the tip of my fingers. After folding it, I put it back on the table. 'Perhaps you wanted to reach the hangman's noose via me.'

'And you did not hesitate to give me shelter in your house?'

'Yes, by now you must have found out what kind of crazy people live in this house.'

And what do you think? Is it that easy to have a peek into a human soul? Maybe, like the old man, the sub-inspector, who had planned to commit suicide after setting the cats free, this was my way to court death.

'Let me say...' I look at Mir without batting my eyes, 'I gave you such an excellent opportunity, and you wasted it. What stopped you that day?'

'I don't know. Perhaps the easier a thing is, the more difficult it becomes.'

I study his face deeply. 'You may be right. Perhaps it was hard for both of us to know each other. Do you know, in the course of handling your case, as also all these years that we have been living under the same roof, every time I thought about you, I would ask myself, what was it that forced you to kill your wife and child? It was not that you were living in hell, and they were also a part of it, dying every day bit by bit. You had definitely not committed the crime to save them from this hell. I don't believe that you didn't know that there were other people involved in this whole nasty thing who were no less responsible for what happened that day, or perhaps this entire society was responsible. You were associated with a political movement, right? You were living with a dream that young people like you would bring about a just society; you wanted to change everything. God knows how many people had been killed on both sides, how many had lost their lives. But did it change anything, or did it affect your political bosses at all? Their statues are still there at the crossroads. Are they not remembered with reverence? So, tell me, where do your wife and child figure in this? I can never understand this paradox. And let me confess as a lawyer, that this question rears its ugly head every day in my life, that when a crime is committed, why does it become difficult to pinpoint the place where the matter might have originated? The world only sees the man standing at the crime scene. Perhaps the police and court have no other option but to make an example of somebody. Perhaps the ritual of human sacrifice is still going on in some form or other so that human society can be saved from an impending gloom, and this is the newest form of ritual we human beings have devised.'

'Perhaps you are right. But it is not possible for a man to go through all these finer points, even though the brain of a man is bigger in proportion to his body compared to other animals. We live our lives so carried on by time that we either end up reconciling to it or try to escape its tentacles with whatever means at our disposal. Every action of ours is born out of some kind of impulse. Perhaps we don't have the capacity to turn back and look very far or look at the epicentre of a thing, or the matter is so complicated, or maybe there is such chaos that we always fail to take the right direction.' He stares at me after placing his hand on his chest. His lips are quivering. 'But as far as I am concerned, I can talk about myself more realistically, keeping in mind those six years that I have spent in prison. They gave me a rare opportunity to peek into my soul. Those were the days when, in my dreams, some wolf would always be hunting a deer. I had been reading a lot of books about animals that I had a habit of bringing from the prison library. You might not know that when a wolf follows a herd, he does not try to become an example of bravery. He is as cowardly an animal as his prey; it's just that he doesn't want to take any risk for himself. So, what does he do? He goes after the weakest member of a herd, someone who isn't fast enough or energetic enough to run very long. Perhaps my wife and children were those weak animals. And the wolf that I would see in my dreams wasn't anyone else but me.'

'You tried to commit suicide. Wolves don't do such things.'

'And, I too, couldn't. Perhaps I was worse than a wolf.' He picks up his suitcase. 'I am taking something with your permission.'

I look at him with a questioning gaze.

Mir whistles. Jhabra's head appears at the door.

'I am glad to see that Jhabra is alive. I had presumed him dead. By the way, it is you who have taken care of him, who saved his life twice. He is your dog from every point of view. You don't need my permission.'

'No, this animal is the property of this house. I can't take him without your permission.'

'You have worked here for so many years. I owe you a great deal of money. Let me calculate the sum and pay it to you.'

'Consider it your fee for my case.' Mir tries to force a smile. He bends on his knees and caresses Jhabra's neck. 'When I set my eye on him for the first time, his body was covered with wounds. He was standing in a drain buried in muck up to his neck to save himself from the blistering sun. That day, I saw my god die in his eyes. So far as my salary is concerned, I am taking a very precious thing from you in the form of Jhabra.'

'I will still keep the money in your account. You can come any day and take it. Or if you may give your address over the phone, I will see to it that it is sent to you.'

He doesn't reply. Kaku and I follow him to the veranda. The dog follows him and descends the stairs. There is no collar around his neck. The recent incident when he almost died again has changed the look of his eyes. There is an obliquity in them. Perhaps he has looked death eye to eye.

'You have forgotten to put a collar on him,' Kaku reminds him.

'I am not his owner.' Mir looks at Kaku with affection. 'Take care of Chandan. He is an angel. This world perhaps doesn't deserve to have a boy like him. He will always be in my mind. Why don't you admit him in a music school? That's the only thing that will keep him alive.'

'What will he earn after learning music? There is only one music school in the city, where they teach Rabindra Sangeet or percussion. The teachers there are themselves novices and teach students only the rudiments of do re mi on the harmonium. Only female students go there. It helps them rope in good spouses.'

'I have a few friends in Kolkata. I will talk to them. They might figure out something for Chandan. It might be that even after learning music, he will live a life of need and hunger. But at least a child who is trying to grow up won't have to die before his time.'

Mir stops at the gate. He is lost in some thought. Is there something else on his mind?

'Take care of yourselves,' he says and leaves.

Kaku closes the gate and returns to my chamber, where I am in my chair again. I have kept the knife inside the drawer. It's a valuable souvenir for me.

'What will you do now?' Kaku asks a strange question.

'I will stay alive,' I say. 'Please send in the visitors. And please look for someone who can replace Mir.'

'I know a widow. She may turn out to be a good caretaker of the house. She lives under a tree inside the government hospital. Her son and daughter-in-law have kicked her out of the house.'

'No woman. I want a man.'

Kaku stands still. I don't look at him.

'My apprehension that day about Mir was not wrong,' he says.

'You can't understand these things. Send in the visitors.'

All my visitors are gone. Kaku is asleep in his chair with his nose on the table. Nripen is nowhere. I am tired without doing anything. Mir must have prepared my lunch, but I am not hungry. I climb the stairs and reach the terrace. The roof of the Chinese Mansion is gleaming in the sun. There is a stockpile of dried leaves in its spines and gutters. The wooden ornamentation at the gables has come loose, looking crooked and misshapen. They have become dilapidated and weak after braving storms and rain all these years. They are in urgent need of repair unless the owner of the Chinese Mansion is as crazy as me. Some birds are circling in the sky. The wind breaks their circle time and again. The birds don't take much time to restore the loop. A stone's throw from the terrace, trees lie uprooted on one side of the road. Their trunks are being pruned with ropes tied to their branches. The shouts of workers boom through the air. The din makes us realize what kind of world is ours. Although the river can't be seen from here as the clumps of trees stall the view, I am sure that its water level must have gone down. The boat that was afloat yesterday, with its sail fluttering in the air, must have been grounded by now, lying face down somewhere in the bank. I take my hands off the railing to go back into the house when a window in the topmost floor of the Chinese Mansion is flung open. Nothing happens for a while. Then a white hand dangles out. It's a young girl, whose hair at the front has been done up with such a vigorous comb that it has lent her forehead a bulging look. The corners of her eyes are traced upward with the help of an eyeliner. As she arranges some coloured stones in the flowerpots that hang outside in iron loops, her eyes meet mine. There is a cat-like glimmer in them. She pulls in the shutters and closes the window.

Siddique Alam was born in Purulia, West Bengal, in 1952 and is currently based in Kolkata. He began writing fiction in 1972, and has since emerged as one of the foremost voices of modern Urdu prose, with five collections of short stories, five novels and a collection of poems, as well as several other stories published across key literary magazines across India and Pakistan. Alam's work is marked by a rigorous attention to historical detail, which he combines with a fantastical and magic realist approach, marking a new trend in Urdu fiction. His work has been translated into Hindi, and several of his short stories have appeared in English translations in *Words Without Borders*, *River of Flesh and Other Stories* (Speaking Tiger Books, 2016) and *Contemporary Urdu Short Stories from Kolkata* (Niyogi Press, 2023). A collected translation of his short stories, *The Kettledrum and Other Stories* by Musharraf Ali Farooqi won the prestigious Armory Square Prize, and was published in December 2024 by Open Letter Books.

Jaideep Pandey is a research scholar in Comparative Literature. He works on idioms of literary modernities, desire, and gender across Urdu, Persian, Arabic and Hindi. His translations have appeared in *The Journal of Urdu Studies*, *Rusted Radishes*, *Indian Literature*, and in two volumes published by Routledge and Oxford University Press. His translation of Sameena Nazir's 'Kallo' won the 2024 Mozhi Prize for Translations from Indian Languages.